Chapter One:

Hidden Secrets

All alone Ashton and Evy sat in the study as rain poured heavily on the manor drenching it. Ashton tried to peek out through the nearly impossible window above the armoire that lit the tiny one window room.

Climbing up on stacked boxes, leading up to the ceiling in the shape of cardboard stairs. Papers flew every where when he slipped on an old rotted cookbook, tumbling to the floor with a loud and obnoxious thud.

Evy frantically freaked out and rushed to Ashton's side to make sure he was okay. With a croak of laughter that echoed through the walls, he sat up and rubbed his head and butt with a bit of a funny bone pain. Evy helped him up and walked him to the aging dirt brown sofa.

Evy looked back to where Ashton landed. She heard a crack as the carpet sank into the floor leaving immense creatures under it's material.

Evy began to cross the little room to investigate. Ashton grabbed her arm and pulled her back to where he was sitting. He suggested they get some flashlights.

Evy skipped over to a small oak desk, next to the sofa, sliding the drawers open. She reached into the dark hollow space. reaching further to retrieve the flashlights. Before she could move her hand fast enough, something started to crawl up it. She jerked her hand back in a yelp of a scream and noticed that it wouldn't let go. She struggled to get it off.

Ashton wobbled over to her, still a little sore from the fall, grabbed the creature off of her so she would stop being so panicked. Only to find out it was a skeleton key with a lavender ribbon entwined in a bow at the bottom. At the edge of the ribbon a white little mouse was caught in it's clutches. It was Alfie their pet mouse. Struggling to breathe and get it's freedom back. Ashton unraveled the ribbon around Alfie's neck, placing the small creature in his pocket. As Ashton and Evy marveled at the key. They heard a scream of anger coming toward the study. Toward them. In a fright they grabbed the flashlights and removed the carpet. Ashton and Evy gawked at the crevassed trap door at the edge of their feet. It was now or never. They grabbed the rusty old door knocker ring and pulled as if their life depended on it.

Page 3.

Chapter Two;
Pain With No Pleasure?

About to descend, Evy drenched the maroon carpet over the back of the secret door and closed it behind them as they descended the steep stairs.

Ashton went first being the braver one in case his sister lost her balance and tumbled down to the bottom with a bruised cut ontop of her red headed scalp. How tragic that would be. But despite their differences, they were all they had in these hard times.

She had always been there for him, even when he was younger. That's why he was so fond of her and loved her. She was his best friend since their shared birth.

He scratched his head with the tip of the flashlight, deep in thought. He barely noticed how dark the walls were.

Evy closed the hatch behind them and as she grasped the stone walls for balance. She sliced her middle fingertip on something sharp. She noticed how her blood poured endlessly, lighting up and changing the dark dreariness' of the place into an ebony lit thriving place. The walls started to move in and out as if they were taking their first breath of fresh air.

Frightened Evy grabbed Ashton by the shoulder to stop his next step. Not knowing that one more step he would have fallen down the swift looking virtical hole embarking deep into the shallow abyss. He turned toward her with an Oh my goodness look about his face that soon turned to gratefulness.

He then noticed the color coming from her fingers that bounced off the walls making everything light up. Evy sat her left hand on the wall beside her, relaxing her weight. Unfortunatly it was so old that it was unable to hold her up for very long. Inches, before she made a nose dive, into the dirt floor, Ashton grabbed her and hauled her back to her feet. She grabbed him and almost strangled him with her grateful and happy hug. Till he tapped her on her arm and said. "Aaaaaiiirrrrrrrrr, Evy I need Air!" With a step back and a large sigh. "Oh. Sorry Ashton, are you okay?" sucking in Oxygen as if his life depended on it. Because it did. "Yeah I'm fine". Then they proceeded through the ragged archway.

Into the misty old Cavern.

The whole cavern itself looked as if somebody got bored and dug a little tunnel into the earth. Deciding to make this their home base.

The Cavern was rounded and the ceiling was at least 20 feet high above Ashton and Evy's head. At the other end there was a door cracked open and light was illuminating the cavern they were in.

They were half way across when they heard a loud cracking sound echoing through the cavern to their ringing ears. Down they descended, into an underground rushing river and over a raging waterfall into a black hole falling into the shallow abyss.

Chapter Three;
New wonders.

Alone in the dark. Evy awoke with her head throbbing and a sense of dizziness that made her eyes feel as though they were going to swell and burst. Instead of worrying about herself, Evy was being overwhelmed with a feeling of dread for her brother, where was he?

Sitting up with a pain in her side, Evy managed to pull her auburn curly locks back in a ponytail. Evy managed to stand tall and straiten the bottom of her skirt to where it sat comfortably above her knee's.

Taking in a deep breath, Evy's eyes wandered around. Evy realized She was on an enchanted island. Green leafs hung everywhere.

Beneath her, pure white sand and the

crystal blue water at the edge of her feet took in sparkles from the sky. On Evy's right was an enormous waterfall embedded in jungle plants. It almost took her breath away as She exhaled and inhaled a couple of times more before spotting the sky. Deep royal blue cascading the black space. Stars scattered in their own little spaces, high above Evy's wandering eyes. Evy looked down at her shoes, making sure her legs were unharmed, and ready for the long trek. Before She would embark on her own little journey to her twin brother. Evy reached into her sky blue sweater and found a flashlight hanging in her pocket. She shook the water from the flashlight and pressed the button.

"Click!"

At first it didn't work. Then Evy shook it again, pressing the button in hopes it would work to light her way.

"Click!"

Not realizing where It was pointed, Evy's eyes were blindsided by the light. She quickly rubbed her eyes with her cotton white shirt. After waiting for the blur to depart, which came quickly. Evy was now ready for the journey. The jungle was very thick with brush and filled with silence. Too silent for her comfort level. Somehow Evy was managing at her own pace.

Page 8.

She glanced up at the stars knowing they would help light her way and give her some hope for the future.   Up ahead Evy saw a clearing and noticed a camp with fire and decided to go and investigate. Reaching the camp, She noticed a sign stating where she was. The camp was empty with not a soul around. Food still sizzled on the fires, everything else was abandoned.

Reaching the sign reading it out loud.

"Eldor!"

Assuming that this world was called Eldor. A draft of wind spilled past Evy and gave chills up her spine leaving hairs trickling up and down her arms. Flooded by unforgiving emotion. At that moment the world called Eldor felt cold and lonesome. It seemed as though there was not a creature of existence there. Evy knew that she could not be alone in this god foresaken place, that shouldn't exist. It appeared to be dark and misty with a creepy mystical breeze that soon fell into fog that was absolutely seemingly to become so thick you could cut into it with the blade of Embala. That was an odd thought, what the heck is the blade of Embala, where did that word come from, humn.. The fog reminded Evy of how wonderfully thick and yummy mothers special recipe of butterscotch cake tasted, boy She missed her so much that Evy felt a breakdown on the verge of releasing salty warm tears from her eye crevices.

So as hard as Evy might try, She kept herself from crying. Plus the fog was almost as thick as barbed wire. which made no difference where she was about to go. Evy looked to both sides of her and realized, she was filled full of wretched thoughts that mortified her. How can she be absolutely alone, Evy knew she had to stop breathing so rough. She could easily throw herself into a panick attack. Evy could hear the faint over crowded voices that filled her mind with what it should have been, if there were people there. She decided to scout around a bit for some unmistakable clues. Found none that caught her interest until, she saw something in the far distance that seemed to be blowing in the wind. Fighting for it's freedom to be united to itself, by begging for the hard, cold, wet mosh pit of the gravel to let it go.

Evy hurried to it as to make sure it wouldn't leave without her first getting a good glimse of it for some sort of answers.

Evy bent down to reach her hands toward the folded up object, to be surprised when it started to glow and shake, then transform itself into the different shades of the rainbows anatomical amazing colors.

It turned bright red then a strange sound fell upon it that threw a shudder of freight through her body and led shivers up her spine.

How was Evy to know that what she touched would come at her like nothing she'd seen before. The wind started to shift and to her dismay a growling sound began to get louder as if it knew she were there, waiting for something to happen. Evy dropped the paper and when she reached down to retrieve it, something leapt onto her.

When Evy hit the ground and rolled a couple of steps away from where she stood, she laid there for a moment to catch her breath. As Evy laid there for a moment longer, she couldn't help but stare up into her peach colored eyelids until she could conjure up enough courage to peek out and see what was afoot.

One eyelid slid open with no problem but the other one seemed to take an eternity to wedge open.

Chapter Four:
Shocking Revelations

When Evy finally opened them, she realized that something was wrong. she wasn't where she was supposed to be. Evy was in a bed, the smell of brewed up stew hovering over her head.

Just then someone rushed in, skirt flaunting about the room as if it was the only thing that mattered.

When Evy saw them, her vison began to blur. All she could see was that the person was a grey blurry shadow wondering around the room with they're back toward her. Evy gathered up her energy, sat up and asked where she was.

The person must have heard her, because they froze in a still shocked position. Then turned and looked her directly in the eyes and vanished into thin air.

Page 12.

Evy took'n back by what she had just seen, screamed. she couldn't believe what she had just seen.

Then a bunch of rogue looking guy's wondered in. There concerned eyes let her know that they were worried about her. Evy blew off the earlier scene thinking they might ponder the idea that she was nuttier then a fruitcake, and she wouldn't blame them. Evy was starting to think one too many screws were loose in her noggin. She shrugged to let them know she was okay, which let them know she was just startled by her surroundings.

Five men stood in front of her in the arched frame of the door. One in the center with two guards on each side of him in matching uniforms. Red balloon shaped drawers and a black sash wrapped around their waste with a dagger in the between the skins of their sash and bare sides.

The man in the middle was dressed in silks as bright as the sunset in the brisk of fall. He had golden bracelets covering both semi-muscular arms. His hair was as dark and silky as the english channel shimmering with the stars on a sweet summer night. His eyes were magnanimous as they glimmered with disposition under the dim candle light. His face was chiseled in a soft but charming way.

He paced back and forth as if he

Page 13.

had ants in his pants and his eyes creased as worry drenched his very eye sockets. He started giving orders to his guards. They gave him an acknowledging nod and left in a light and quick pace. After they left he turned toward Evy and started talking in some rubbish language she couldn't quite calculate quick enough for his patience. He stopped, pointed at her and said something that sounded like

"Froodinophkli eh prucheska flankritcha?"

Then glided smoothly toward her and touched her forehead with the palm of his right hand, his left hand he placed under her breast bone while closing his eye's. The places he touched started to glow and tingle with a warm feathery feeling. After what seemed like a long five seconds he removed his hands and slid onto the edge of the bed and said once more.

"Hello Princess, We have waited an Eternity for you to show up here"

Evy covered her eyes with her hands but couldn't relinquish the fact that her mouth lay gaped open like a nutcrackers wooden mouth.

"We almost gave up on the foretold prophecy that you would come and save our prospering little tribe."

After hearing that, Evy removed her hands and slid them down her face to rest upon her blanketed lap.

Page 14.

"What are you talking about?" Evy asked in horror

"Where am I and when am I, Who are you?"

Losing her cool, she began to panic. Not only was she lost, but these nut jobs put a weight on her shoulders, Evy didn't think she would be able to bare. This time the man on the end of the bed sat straight up and softened his expression to understand how she was feeling and placed his hand on her knee and repeated slowly so that she not miss a word.

"My Name Is Sire Ahckmelutra, Heir to Embala."

Then he pulled an Ancient dust packed book out from behind him and cracked it open to read to her. Times are dark and lonely. When in the year of Neuel. A strong and powerful woman will immaculate with the sense to stay and combine the world of Embala into one sacred place. She will be beautiful and intelligent and every creature will want to follow her. She will choose between two men which she will marry one and decide the fate of all.... One who competes for her love and affection will be the sire of Embala and the other shall be the Sire of Showknizar.

With that information Evy lay back against the silky lavender goose feather pillow and let out a sigh of anguish.

"So you some how think that I am the one in that prophecy?"

Page 15.

Evy said in a soft but hasty tone. "Yes I believe you are, we found you laying in the field by a dead tree as old as time itself. Laying half in the river and half embarked on the gravel. Since we've brought you to my palace, I have grown quite fond of you while you sleep."

He said as his eyes lit up.

"Ah, I see you have been mistaken. I am lost and need to get home and quick. My mother is probably sick with worry and crying her eyes out as we speak." Although what Evy said was probably true, she knew that even if she went back. Evy was to be wed to Sir Henry Lockhart. Although charming he might have been. she's certainly not ready to just settle down with anybody. her wishes were to seek adventure and settle in the states. Evy certainly had no clue how to get out of this tangling web. "Princess may I enquire about your name?"
He asked so politely that She couldn't refuse a man of his stature.

"My Name Is Lady Evy Trinity Bridgewater"

As Evy said that she heard the room echo in delight at it. He slid closer to her and asked her to merry him. Out of panic, Evy rushed an answer. "Sire Ahckmelutra, I would be honored and delighted to accept your grand invitation,

Page 16.

but I would like some time to register all that has happened to me today."

With that answer, he shook his head in response and said as kind as he could without cracking his face.

"I understand your disposition and will grant you a month, no less and no more, and when you are done taking in your surroundings. I will merry you with or without your consent. You will be mine to win this aweful heart breaking war, and to do with as I please."

With that he slid off of the bed, bowed at her and vanished out the arched door way. Evy paused and rewound the strange encounter and replayed it through her mind over and over till she crashed down on her pillow's and slept for what felt like an aweful eternity

Page 17.

Chapter Five;
Attempted Escape.

The next morning Evy awoke with dread in her gut and couldn't help but wonder what would become of herself.

The sun was about to come through the wilted curtains of the huge room. Without hesitation, Evy gathered some of her belongings and a long sheet. Tying the sheet to a metal post near the window, Evy threw it out and descend it.

The sheet slid down the side of the castle missing the ground by four feet. Easily she slides down like a pro. She hits the ground and rolls a couple of feet. After getting up from the soft grass, an alarm sounds and guards start to give chase to her.

Evy see's a patch of forest about a yard away from her.

Page 18.

As Evy's running, she hears Sire Ahckmelutra yelling her name, glancing back over her shoulders, The sky is horrifically diminished by angry clouds. Electricity filters through the sky, igniting a tree or two on fire as it eats them from the inside out leaving nothing but burnt chaos behind in it's wake.

Almost to the tree's as She stumbles into a man who is tall and broad. With a smile on his face, as Evy gathers up her dropped belongings and apologize. His eyes shinning emerald and his silken hair glistening in the storm. With her stuff in her arms, Evy begins to run, but a hand grabs her wrist and prevents her from continuing her quest for freedom.

Evy struggles with the person kicking and fighting until he let's go. Stumbling back in a painful tumble down through tree's perched along the hill hitting every branch, crook and nanny. Til the ground breaks her fall and a rock becomes her pillow, then all goes blank.

The world removes itself from Evy and her conscious is soaring in the dream realm leaving her behind.

Page 19.

Chapter Six;
Who Am I?

When Evy awoke, her head was hurting and it felt as though it was going to implode. her eyes were a bit blurry.

As Evy pulled herself together and started to sit up. She reached her head up and felt something trickle down her forehead. Evy grazed her fingertip up against the liquid on her forehead gently and was in wonder at what it was.

Then looking up and around to see her surroundings. The first thing she saw was a big wide range of trees and forest. Evy looked to the ground behind where her head lay when she became conscious. There was a sharp rock with blood smeared around it.

Taking a quick glance back at her fingertips, she realized in a matter

Page 20.

seconds that it was her blood that was coming from the opened wound.

Evy moved her eyes up again and noticed that there was a steep hill and broken branches that led down it toward her bestilled body.

Knowing she had to get up and find her way to a near by village or toward safety, to get her wound tended. So when Evy stood up, fighting off the dizziness. she had to figure out how to get out of the woods that looked all the same from all different directions. Proceeding to brush off her lavender dress and pull the filthy, sticky, weeds out of her dark auburn hair. Evy chose and she did so very quickly. (Due North West) or was it East? While Evy was walking, she had to figure out what her name was and fast to keep people's suspision from rising. her memory started to become clearer little by little. Right out of the blue, she picked a name, It was more of an Estimation. Her name from now on was to be Evy, until she could figure out who she really was.

The more Evy tried to think about it, her head was sent reeling with heavy thudding. her name wasn't going to be enough. If they asked about her last name or even where she came from she would not have an answer. What if they asked her why she wears a fancy dress fit for a princess? Evy hummed to herself while in concentrated thought.

Page 21

Chapter Seven;

Admirable Rescue.

While Evy was contemplating her current issues, she almost tripped on a rock near a pathway or road made of rocks and stones. Looking left then right, she decided to cross.

When getting in the middle of the road, Evy could feel the ground shaking and horses squeeling, Then "Yah!!" echoed to her. All she could do was freak out, standing there as still as a stone, as the carriage came closer to her.

Having only a fraction of a second to get out of the way or become as flat as a stone in the pathway beneath her feet.

Then suddenly out of no where, A dark cloaked

Page 22.

figure plucked her out of the road, where the carriage would have flattened her into morning porridge. Placing Evy on the back of the sattled black stallion saying nothing to her.

Chapter Eight;
Orientations for fools.

The ride was bumpy and made her jittery, to the point she felt nausious. It seemed like an eturnity. Looking around to catch her breath and glance in her surroundings.

They soon stopped near a waterfall; that the very glimse of it made Evy shutter, it was the most breath taking natural monument she's ever seen. Almost indescribable.

The figure hopped off of his sturdy old black stallion. Then he turned to help her off by the waist. Thinking if she got a good glimpse of her rescuer then she would give him a proper thank you.

After setting her down on the ground, The cloaked figure pulled off the hooded attire,

Page 24.

which covered who he really was. Evy's Jaw dropped and all she could get out of her mouth was a whimper. He looked at her with Emerald Eyes and gave off a coy little smile and said with an accent so strong, Evy felt every bit of her body melt. "Are you okay miss, What is your name lass?" Evy shuttered and realized that she was being Acknowledged. Her cheeks turned aflame as she blushed with Emberrassment and her hands started to sweat. Then Evy said

"Yes, I'm fine. Thank you so much dear sir, for saving my life from that horrid carriage., My name Is Evy". He looked at Evy with a cool contempt, then proceeded with the questions.

"Where do you hail from lady Evy?"

With a nervious glance back at his angelic face she said

"I'm Not sure."

Was all Evy could muster the energy to whisper. she desperatly hoped he wouldn't ask anymore questions.

He pulled all his strength together not to ask many questions because he was a man who rather liked small talk and dreaded the long boring converstations.

Page 25.

Even though it killed him inside to restrain from touching her creamy white flesh and holding her lovingly.

Then slightly he tried to pronounce his name so that the lady could understand him through his strong unrecognizable thick accent and get his name right. "M'Lady the names Aiden McTavish"

He turned away from Evy and started to walk fast into the Abyss of the forest. As he left she thought to herself, how awkward that first greeting was with him and smiled to herself, then began to build camp and gather wood for the fire.

For a while Evy pondered a thought on why his accent seemed so lush and familiar. Flickers of her life back home cursed through her thoughts. His accent was a borderline between Scottish, and Irish. When they're eyes met before, she felt a click. A belonging. her thoughts were muddled. She felt like she had met him before on unknown circumstances. A perposterious Idea, but none the less Evy reveled in it.

Page 26.

Chapter Nine;
Unscheduled Disasters

It didn't take long to figure out, Evy had no food to cook or satisfy her stomach's endless growling.

Then it dawned on her, why would any animal live in these woods. There hasn't been an ounce of food anywhere, since she's been introduced to the cold, harsh temperature of the outdoors.

As soon as Evy was done putting up the tent she heard hard footfalls echoing throught the little camp area, coming toward the tent. A thought crept right up on her through the shivers of her spine.

What if those foot falls weren't the nice, handsome gentleman who had just a few hours ago rescued her from that run away carriage. What if it were someone entirely

Page 27.

different trying to raid the supplies and bring her harm.

Thats when Evy had to think and do so very quickly. Turning to see what was surrounding her in the tent. Her eyes bounced from object to object as her heart raced.

Then Evy found something that could be of some use to her.

"A Fire Poker"

Not very scary, but enough to stun the intruding attacker, so that she could make a run for it and pray that her rescuer would lend a helping hand to her second escape.

Evy reached for the object but was too late. Suddenly she was spun around so fast that her head was trying to catch up.

When It finally caught up, She soon realized what was going on. she was wrapped in someone's arms and on the dirt floor being wrestled. Evy couldn't believe what was happening. Was at a total struggle to get unhandled.

She then saw a tall dark shadowy figure off one of the tent walls.

"Thunk!!!"

She began to get dizzy with lack of oxygen, her eyelids began to weigh her face down. Then she was out.

Page 28.

Chapter Ten;
  Frights go bump

The dream Evy was thrust into was wierd although she's had many. Couldn't quite remember them all, but this one was embedded in her cranium. It was dark and hazy with a castle in the wide outskirts of it.

Yet someone would be calling her name from a high tower above the clouds.

Their voice was muffled and their face was a big blur. From what Evy could tell It was a man reaching for her and the sky going pitch black with eccentric colors not found anywhere she's ever been.

Page 29.

Chapter Eleven;

Dreams of wakening love?

When Evy awoke, she could smell an unrecognizable fragrance burning.

Her eyes were yet again blurry but soon adjusted. she could hear someone chanting. A voice she's never heard.

Beginning to sit up but when she try's her side begins to burn and ache. Once again she's puzzled about her where abouts.

The room is dark with only one small chamber door. Having a warm kind of cozy feeling about it.

Behind that stunning door Evy could hear rough foot falls coming toward the room she was laid up in. They were quick and fast paced. The person coming

Page 30.

toward her was breathing so heavy that the breathing almost sounded un-human. The door cracked and the figure stepped inside the dark and musky room. Evy's jaw dropped as she immediately recognized the guest. It was Aiden, her earlier rescuer. "Aiden Mctavish". His smile was reassuring as it lit up his face as he spotted her acknowleding his very adventurous presence. When he smiled a jolt of heat rushed through her veins and her cheeks flustered as red as blood on snow.

Aiden walked with elegance and adventure in each and every wonderous step. Bent low and placed his left hand on the nape of her neck and his right hand on her lower back. Lifting her closer to his heated body. His Emerald Eyes sizzling with passion. Reaching his tender lips down on her's. A jolt of electricity unlocked a secret barrier surrounding Evy's placid heart all while making her knee's go weak. The kiss was soft and full of vigorous passion making her feel like she was about to swoon. All that surrounded them began to fade and swirl. Without hesitation her arms reached up cradling his neck pulling him closer. His chest sitting firm and warm against her bossoms. their hearts beating as one. Evy's hair dangling through his muscular fingers down her back. She suddenly felt light headed and their bodies began to float lighter than being on a sweet summer rain cloud in a breeze.

 Another jolt of electricity and everything that she clung to gets ripped from her grasp.

Page 32.

The Title Of A Crucified Innocence

Chapter Twelve;
Untidy Events

The cage rattled Evy awake like someone poured icy cold water on her. The wagon beneath the poorly built cage trotted across steep crevices on a trail of earth and sharp pebbly gravel. Evy's surroundings startled her. Sliding up to a sitting position.

The Lavender gown she was wearing, torn to shredded ribbons barely covering her modest ample body.

Evy's hair, frazzled and contorted in webs descending her scalp. Dried blood seeping crusty paths down the nape of her neck. Where a cold sweat remoistened it and dampened the shredded gown sitting

Page 33.

comfortably on her sweaty curves. Like sticky hunny from bee's. Closing her lids. Evy rested her fingertips on her forehead slowly rubbing down toward her eye sockets. Holding her hands firmly yet steady covering her face. (Where Am I Now?) Evy pushed her hands up again to slide the loose strands of hair out of her face and behind her scalp. Evy Glanced around the empty space between herself and the bars. The floor must've been constructed out of dirt, wood paneling, rotted out bars, and last but not least, A dirty brown rug of some sort with a multitude of stains. The corner opposite of Evy sat a metallic dish bowl full of muddy liquid, she assumed was water. Looking at her hands finally noticing the weight of jingling chains wrapped around her bleeding wrists. The links entangled in a web descending toward her ankles and then toward a set of bars above the dish bowl. Hyde of some animal wrapped around the outer area of the bars barely letting any light in from the sunny outdoors. Knowing that seeing the outside was inevitable. Feeling a comforting breeze was wishful thinking as the leaves of wild oaks and fields of yellow vegitations giggled as the wind tickled by. Knowing that she would never escape to see her brother Ashton or their home ever again. The recognizable feeling Evy came to acknowledge as

Page 34.

every day chitter. Doubt, Fearing her hopes dashed down to being lost and alone, to feeling numb and paranoid with fear. A sudden halt dragged the wagon to a stop, thwarting Evy into the bar's making her head burn with stinging rage that blurred her eyes until tears drenched her face. Peeking out of one of the slits on the animal hyde. The outer area felt darker, like death had conquered all, resting in his new home. The clouds darkened over the hazy sun as it dipped fervently behind moss covered hills and oaks soaked with dew in the distance.

Relinquishing a dark blanket of soft stars and rigidly dangerious clouds. Even the moon hid in fright.

The cage jolted a couple of times as a thin muscular man diddled and cursed at the knotts and locks on the cage.

He wore a loins cloth. His hair so black it gave off a shimmering blue tint relaxing on his lower darkened back. His eyes were fierce like a hawk's. Dark and menacing like empty space. Coyly tame at certain times like a king of lions.

After the locks and knotts finally let loose, he gave off a sigh of relief. His muscles tensed as he slid the cage door open, grabbing the links to Evy's chains and pulling ferociously. Falling forward out of the back of

Page 35.

the wagon's end. Evy almost nose dived onto her face inches from the dirt.

His arms caught Evy in a warm embrace, she almost felt safe if not for the chains, blood, head ache, and cage. Setting Evy down on the ground, he began to examine her with eyes intent on examining his prized victim. Before removing his arms completely, his hands slid down her back and over her firm bottom resting on her outer thigh's, making Evy feel uncomfortable. Bending her sideways as if trying to kiss her at the end of a slow dance. Lifting Evy's right thy against his bare skinned leg up his waist as his fingers caress in a circular motion rising a powerful sensation tingling up her dingy peach colored arms. Evy's vision show'd sparks as she felt them explode inside of her corneas. After a few seconds, she was frightened he was going to do something truly savage. "Ripppp!!"

Evy's gown's cry's, echoed through the empty air Taking a huge chunk from her gown. He Placed it over her eyes. Spinning Evy around so that her arched back faced him. After tying the wilting material, he placed his hands on her shoulders. Pulling her back closer to his heated body. Sliding his palms down her forearm past her guilded wrists over her knuckles to the chain. A groan escaped his parted lips reaching her ears.

Holding that pose for a moment longer.

Page 36.

Spinning her around once again, dragging Evy behind him. Like a dog on a leash. Pulling her along a yard or two. Stopping, too swiftly pick her up, so she wouldn't delay his patience. His arms were warm and tight. Evy's head felt a bit groggy and heavy on her shoulders. All she could do was lie her head back and wait until they stopped and she'd get some answers No matter how frightning they might be. When her head made contact with his chest, a groan silent but rumbling, burrowed from his chest to his lips as he tried to hide it with a cough. They must have been on stairs because the ride was bumpy. Lightning scattered over the rigid clouds letting rain begin to pour heavily.

When reaching the top of the stairs, he sat her down. As Evy's feet hit the ground, a thunderious lightning bolt hit between them.

Evy wasn't sure which she was more afraid of. The man or etched hairs climbing up her back. Knowing she couldn't see, never stopped her from making a run for it. As Evy was running from shock, she couldn't hear the foot fall's closing in the distance behind her. In the next moment a hand grasped a huge chunk of her hair and yanked her back into locked arms. Evy thought hard about resisting. In the end, she knew, she chose the right decision.

Page 37.

With her heart racing, water drenching Evy like a moist sheet. Rain washed away the sweaty heat pounding away from every pore of her life form. She wasn't sure if the man holding her was the same one who dragged her up the stairs. While they were standing there another set of feet started to walk toward Evy from behind, then passing fervently, splashing through the little puddles. As they got a couple of feet in front of her they turned, and walked two or more steps then stopped.

A jingling sound came from the halted person when he wrestled with the solid object. Evy assumed was a key hole and keys.

After a few seconds the sounds stopped and a door was cracked open. the creak was so eerie, she began to get flashbacks of an empty, foggy, lonely place that somehow brought tears to her eye's.

Guiding Evy through the misty archway and down a shaft full of rugged stairs. The cement stairs turned in a circular motion. Water seeped from the ceiling and cracks lulling down the walls and stairs leaving tiny rushing rivers from little puddles. Every few steps down, a flash of lighted torches hanging from the walls lit a small path. Steam sizzled as water dripped carelessly onto them. Evy's nose itched and tickled as her hairs in her nose sucked in a puff, full from the stench of death and

Page 38.

heavy smoked meat swelling up her lungs through her out stretched nostrils. Leaving Evy coughing and breathless.

At the last step they stopped. The man behind Evy began to untie the blindfold. When it slid away from her eyes a heavy glaring haze replaced darkness. Ahead of Evy lay a door frame with the door wide open. On the other side was a corridor. The floor was cement and the wood paneling covering the windows letting a glare blind her vision until she could bare it no longer and had to look away.

The floor was as cold as chilling ice. The sun beating on Evy's form was comforting, rushing chills away from her. Filling Evy with warmth and a self of righteousness. As Evy's spirit started to rise, the men behind her pushed her to move foreward.

Page 39.

Chapter Thirteen;

Unplanned Events

At the end of the blinding hall a throne emerged in black shimmering steel. Billions of rays from the windows bounced off of it, making it look like a god sat between it's grasps.

On each side of the throne hung banners of licorice red and golden trim. Black engulfed the center leaving the shadow outline of a sword.

On the floor under the licorice banners stood dozens of candles on each side of the poles. Stairs leading up to the throne were also black as night with gold and red trimming. The threads soft as camel silk and ancient as dinosaur fossil's.

Lining the wall's were men who were dressed in

black balloon shaped drawer's similar to Sire Ahckmelutra's men. That memory came to Evy quickly like the dream. The only difference was the color of bottoms and the fierce eyes and rigid faces full of war and hate.

The corridor was a yard long. Every footstep felt aweful and horribly embarrassing like she was walking down death row to the gallows.

The man on the throne had tinted flames for hair. not yellow and not red, but a sandy beige. Wild and untamed. His face was solid, full of confinement. Eyes as blue as ice. Skin tan and rugged like smooth leathery silk. The whole time Evy was being guided toward him, she had a Dagger at her back. He never moved his eyes off of her. He was leaning on his left elbow and wiggled his fingers in the air for the serf to come to him. When he spoke, it was in hushed tones. Then he waved the young woman away, sending her to do his biddings. He stayed in that same position until Evy arrived at his feet to share an audience with him. she did not speak for fear that he would bring his wrath upon her and have her executed. When he spoke the tone of his words were crueler than his icy eyes. "Ah. I have heard soo much about you Evy that I began to think you were merely a retundant myth."

While scooting closer to the edge of his throne, he looked more dazzling like a creature who couldn't be tamed.

"My name is Sire Iolis, Of Showhizar."

Then he sat up with such conviction that it startled her. Beginning to pace he said.

"I wonder if you know the prophecy, With you by my side we will full fill it and Embala shall be mine."

With that he jumped off of the top of the stairs and grabbed Evy by the back of the neck and pulled her close to his parted lips and his bare chest.

His heart beating with a sense of control and her's racing like a captured animal. Evy's guilded wrists kept her a small distance from being totally consumed by his possessive embrace.

The kiss was warm but also savage. His grip on her ceased, sliding his hands to Evy's shoulders, he pushed her back into the arms of soldiers.

"Take her to her chambers and get her ready for our wedding!"

With that Evy was led to her chambers with such force that her mind was shaken up, Full of confussion.

Page 42.

Chapter Fourteen;
Dreams Gone Wry.

The chamber door slammed shut with such conviction it almost knocked Evy off her feet. Looking around Evy could see three pieces of furniture lay in the chamber. A mirror, a standing stool and a table with drawers. On the table sat a bunch of fine silks as white as spring clouds. Needles poked out of a stuffed red ball as string led a tangling journey across the desk, weaving it's way like a winding stone path. The mirror was shimmering as the sun came through the windows and birds began to chirp. This place seems so strange. When Evy was outside, it was pouring so aweful that she almost believed she was in the Era of Noah and his Magnanimous Arc.

Page 43.

As Evy sat gaping out the parted curtains, the sun was out in bloom. Shining. she didn't notice at first glance, but by this angle she could see why it was so bright. Their were two suns.

The Castle was as black as burning coals. Their were no plants in the courtyard. Only bare dirt and gravel.

A musky scent came rushing past Evy into her chamber. The smell was the best thing to happen to her since her luck turned to crumbles leaving Evy hanging in empty sorrow. The smell was a mix between Ivy and Lavender. While Evy was glaring out the perched window in the tower, she barely noticed that someone had entered. Out of the corner of her eyes she could see them standing at the table rustleing with the material and when evy turned around she realized who it was. It was the serf from earlier who was given orders by the sire. She was pretty and really young. Not much older than the age of sixteen. her hair was sparkling blonde and pulled back in a loose bun, that had some tresses falling out. Her eyes were muddy brown. With a sullen facial expression. She walked with grace and great patience in her grey gown. When she noticed Evy was watching her, she walked over to her. Back immensely straight, taking in long strides.

Page 44.

When she reached Evy, she said not a word and grabbed Evy's hand and began to pull her to the standing stool across the room.

Birds twittered in the distance, Evy stepped up onto the stool and waited for further instructions and body language. So Evy would know what to do next. The girl turned and grabbed a large pair of cutting sheers and walked to Evy, watching Evy for a split second then went around Evy's back to grab a huge chunk off of the bottom of Evy's gown. Cutting upward releasing Evy's dress from it's sweaty grasps. Leaving it lifeless and dead as the wilted material descended toward the floor.

As it fell Evy watched as her naked body was revealed. It must've been along time since seeing her body because she was dirty and bruises covered herself. Evy's side, that always ached was as black and royal blue as a hideous war wound. The blood coming from her head was still seeping. The chains that bound Evy were drenched in blood.

While the girl was working around the dress, she pulled a key out from her apron that would release Evy. The key was familiar. It had a lavender ribbon entwined at the bottom of the sterling silver skeleton. The girl walked to the front of Evy and began to unchain her. Finishing up her last ankle, Evy's muscles were aching as feeling rushed back into them.

Page 45.

With a clank they fell effortlessly onto the floor. Then the girl grabbed the cloth on the table and unraveled it. To Evy's dismay it was a silky white and golden robe. After it was fully secure hiding her modest body. The girl walked to the chamber door. Knocked on it, then behind the door came a clanging sound all too recognizable. Keys clanging, door being released from the archway. The girl moved to the side as three men entered. One with a tub, the others with buckets of steaming hot water the size of their torso's. They glided as if weight didn't matter in their world. Only to stop in the center near where Evy stood. They sat the stuff down with little effort on their part. Then they left without a word. When the chamber door shut behind them, the door let off a locking sound ensuring that Evy wouldn't be able to escape. The girl turned to walk briskly toward Evy. When she arrived at her stopping spot, she pulled a sponge out from behind her back and gave off a coy little smile. When she smiled she had no teeth and no tongue. It was completely severed off. Without hesitation Evy stepped into the piping hot water. Tipping her toe in first to test the temperature, at first the water was soo hot it felt as cold as ice water. But then the steam brought on the redness to Evy's ankles and the heat cursed up her legs and her back.

Page 46.

It was too hot for Evy to bare. she began to hop back out then she saw the girl staring at her with flames incursing her muddy brown eyes. A dagger pointed right at Evy. Her head shook left then right a couple of times before she lipped "Get Inn" pointing the dagger menacingly at the tub. So Evy stayed and bared the hot water because she would rather face heat burning her flesh than having the girl stick that horrible dagger in Evy's back. When Evy sat down, the girl walked over to the table and sat the dagger down to retrieve some bath oils and the recient sponge. After grabbing them the girl slid toward the tub Evy was in and began to mix the oil with the water and the sponge making bubbles that smelled of french lavender and a hint of white whine. The girl wasn't as gentle as Evy'd hoped for. She scrubbed her aching skin leaving more bruises and cracks. Trying to put off the pain Evy began to day dream, then her mind went blank. Everything became as white as milk. All thoughts and events came rushing back to Evy. The first thing that came back was her brother Ashton and Home. Then Aiden was the last thing that crept through Evy's mind leaving her with small kisses and romantic Embraces in her fantasy. A yank and the girl was behind Evy trying to undo her tangling mess of hair descending Evy's scalp leaving more frazzled hairs than Evy thought she had to begin with.

After those torturous moments the girl nudged Evy to get up and out of the bath. So Evy did what the girl told her to do. Evy stood feeling water cascade off of every crevice and bump on her body making her feel like an original waterfall. Hot water steaming off of Evy until the girl wrapped that robe around Evy again to cover up the bruises and her modest innocence. Evy glanced once more to the decorative mirror and saw that her hair was pulled back in a bun and her bruises faded. Evy's eyes were weary and full of dread and her complexion was horrible. Even though she felt no hope, the woman in that mirror, showed Evy that she was hope. Surviving is what she has to do, best in her hopes to find her brother. Evy stood their and waited for orders from her unfortunate new friend with no voice. When Evy recieved no orders of what to do, she looked at her. The girl's back was turned to Evy as she shuffled through the material on the table then her head raised and she spun around, too quick for Evy to question the girl's sudden change in heart. The girl held a dress in her hands. Made of the same material as the robe. White silk with golden trim and a neck line that showed off Evy's cleavage very well. Evy put it on and hoped the girl wouldn't get angry enough at her to toss Evy out the window half naked. The dress fit without needing to be measured.

After that the girl had Evy put on matching slippers made of the same material and sat her down on the stepping stool and began to mess with her hair and put it up in pearl clips and then the girl added a necklace and earrings that matched. Evy watched the girl work fervently and the girl's working, was like watching a genius. She was careful and cautious on how she made Evy's hair look. By the time the girl was done Evy's hair was magnanimous. It was fashioned in a braided bun with one single long curl trailing the nape of Evy's neck down her lower back, Evy had her bangs grazing her cheeks in perfect unicen. When Evy stood up looking into the mirror in wonder, the girl pulled back and grabbed the dagger as if Evy was about to attack her, even though Evy wasn't. Evy's auburn hair glimmered and set off a smile she could not hide. Evy looked Beautiful. While Evy was looking into the mirror she noticed the girl was still staring at her. So Evy tried to hide her smile but, it only made Evy's eyes light up even more and her cheeks go even redder. Evy put her hands over her gaping mouth and felt her lips close ever so slightly. As Evy was staring off into the empty space in the mirror, a realization hit her smack dab in the forehead. "I'm being forced into marriage by some savage king, how am I going to get out of this one?" Not realizing, Evy said that out aloud.

The girl had looked shocked by the information that seeped from Evy's slippery lips. While Evy was in thought while saying those things. Evy had no idea that they're was another person present in the chamber. Evy followed the girls gaze toward the door and found Sire Iolis standing there with shock and anger written all over his face. He did another sign to the silent girl with his hands and she looked down and rushed out as if she would rather be somewhere else. The girl shut the chamber door behind her. When the locking sound ceased, he stepped forward still upset. He began to pace left and right consistantly. Then he stopped and turned back toward Evy. Sun melting off of his face. leaving shadows etched in his ruggid lines. Before anger could consume all of him, a glimmer of passion filled is eyes. After a second of stalling, Evy glanced back at the mirror not realizing that he moved so quick it sent shivers up her spine. He moved behind Evy in a blink of an eye. Grabbing Evy by her throat pulling her closer to his strong chest. All Evy could do was watch as his eyes lit like flames, an angry groan rumbled from his diaphragm, whispering full of passion. "Savage I Am, We'll see how savage you think I am tonight when I've you all to myself." Evy whimpered and tears streaked her face as she could no longer hide her true colors. He glanced from the side of Evy's cheeks, to the mirror she was staring into. Compassion filled his eyes as he sat her down and fled out the locked door.

Chapter Fifteen;
Bells ring, But I dont sing

After he left, Evy looked back at her frightened self in the mirror, wiping her eyes. Smearing what dignity she had left. The sun's began to set leaving the sky dimming with a breathe of fresh air.

Walking over toward the window, looking down at the court yard. Hoping that Evy could escape this mess that she was entangled in. What Evy saw, made her legs shake.

At the bottom, there were dozens and dozens of people and what looked like a ceremony.

Suddenly Evy's head got heavy and the room started to spin making her dizzier than a dog. Evy grasped the window seil for support and slid down to the floor where she sat holding the wall for dear life.

Page 51.

An arm grasped Evy's waist and pulled her upward to a standing position. shaking her, to make sure she was okay.

Evy's eyes were trained on the floor, but she slowly raised her eyes starting from black balloon shaped pants and sash with a golden dagger being held into place by the sash and his skinned waist. Evy's eyes wandered even further up his tan, broad chest and his muscular arms.

Her mouth fell silently open as his neck, jaw bone and eyes looked so familiar.

Page 52.

Chapter Sixteen;
Another Handy Escape
For The Taking.

Without letting Evy speak he guided her toward another wall, pressing her against the tapestry and bookstand.

Voices mingled in the hall coming closer. Having Evy pinned, his chest against hers. Their hearts beating as one. Evy's racing as excitement and passion for this daring man filled her eye sight. Grabbing her wrists and lifting them above her head while moving closer for a more exciting kiss.

When he released Evy's arms, she dropped them to her waist to breathe out a pleasureful sigh.

Page 53.

A loud noise sounded in the hall and the next thing Evy knew, Aiden was leading her through a secret passage in the wall behind the bookstand. Soon it closed behind them and the passage filled with dusty darkness.

He guided Evy by his right palm. The feeling of it was warm and comforting in her left hand,, their fingers tangled together.

They moved fast and carefully not to make a sound and disrupt the commotion going up above and around them. The halls echoed as drips of water seeped from cracks, sweetly falling to the ground leaving small pools behind in their wake. After traveling for a quarter of a mile in this maze, Evy's feet began to ache under the pressure of her body. she didn't know how, but Aiden knew that Evy's feet were pestering her. He stopped quickly. Letting go of her hand to swiftly pick her up, holding Evy like a baby doll. It was sweet and made Evy's heart skip a couple of beats. So trusting this man with her life and even more with her heart, Evy leaned her head back and she felt his heart race and flutter as he whispered…

"Were almost out, I promise my Love."

His vary accent was filling Evy's veins with heat and passion. She longed for him even more than she realized the first time she saw him, when they met by that magnificent waterfall.

Page 54.

Although thinking back, Evy felt as though she's met him someplace else. Every time she tried to think back on those memories, Evy's mind would get hazy filling with a jabbing pain that makes her head wound hurt as though it's being ripped open again. Evy's breathing came in heavy and wheezy. Drowsing off was easy from all the fatigue and stress of the events following waking up in that dreadful cage that made her feel like an animal. Aiden stopped for a second more then sat Evy down on her feet to open another passageway door. This one let light into the darkened tunnel burning her eyes. Evy went to wipe away the tears that started to form from the blinding light, she was stopped by Aiden as he wiped them for her and gave her a kiss while saying in a joyous tone.

"We're out, There's Ithica. We can leave and never Return!"
With that revelation, Evy told him that her brother went missing and he said he understands everything. Aiden led the way into the woods with ressurance. taking Evy to his black steed, which rushed to them at a whisper of a whistle from his soft lips. He placed his firm palms around Evy's waist and lifted her up onto the back of the horse to guide her toward safety. The ride was brisk and left Evy's cheek bones chapped and sore. After riding for a couple of miles, her butt began to get sensitive to the attention the seat was giving her. Just before it got too numb, they stopped

Page 55.

and Aiden helped Evy off like a perfect gentleman.

As soon as her feet hit the ground, Aiden lifted the palm of his hand and smacked the back end of the horse. It stood on it's hinde legs and looked as though it was reaching for the stars. Then galloped off into the brush of the tree's.

After it left, Aiden grasped Evy's hand in his, fingers entwined and heat rushing to her cheeks once more.

Evy didn't notice before, but a small cabin hid under a bunch of tree brush and vines near a little river bank cursing around it. Little pebbly rocks glistened in the sunlight leaving sparks of light illuminating off of the lime branches, while grass surrounded the river.

Page 56

Chapter Seventeen;
        Enveloping Strange Tale's.

Guiding Evy toward the cabin, she was mystified at how adorable and ancient it was.

How are they too conceal it from passer byers?

It was hidden away from the naked eye.

What kind of genius was the person who created it? Questions kept overpowering Evy's cranium. She was trying to sort things out. This place was hidden away from prying eyes. It surprised Evy to the very core. As they walked through the hidden arch way, leaves of green ivy and vines hung

Page 57.

low like a soft sheet keeping shade and protection from leaving.

A cool comfort cascading into the atmosphere. Leaves tickled her cheek as they ducked low and moved them aside. Aiden held Evy's hand with great gentility.

Leading her into a small corridor cut off by a stone spiral stair case. They began to descend at a hasty pace.

At the bottom, Evy slipped and missed the last step and fell slanted into open arms. They lifted her up and sat her back down on solid ground.

Evy lifted her gaze up toward the person holding her. To Evy's surprise, it wasn't Aiden. It was someone entirely different. The outline of the man was all she could see. From what Evy could tell he was wearing all black. Like a robe of some sort. It rustled around his ankles as he stood her up. After removing his palms from around her waist. This man had an intriging smile that blazed as bright as the moon peaking through the dark shadows of the night. Evy found herself dumb struck. Then at the hint and curve of the smile. She noticed a couple of teeth that glinted raiser sharp. Shimmering in the candle lit room.

He turned and led Evy into the next room with Aiden.

"Why aren't you the clumsy one, I hear so much about you."

Page 58.

The room was dark and full of mildew stench that ricochette off of the bricks in the walls and seemed to linger.

The temperature seemed to drop as Evy entered through the arch of the door frame.

The only light that protruded the darkness seemed to come from a Caldron with an icy blue flame frozen in mid air, the rim of the glistening coal black caldron comfortably encircling it like a snug ring. The flames that were frozen in place seemed to give off a soft luminous glow that sent magical waves rippling through the air.

Chapter Eighteen;
Doubts Gone Wry.

The mysterious man guided them toward the caldron. Out of sheer excitemend of seeing something as magical as rippling waves. Evy couldn't resist, reaching out and grasping her fingers around the misty substance. Not knowing what could happen. The oddest sensation spread vigoriously through Evy's limbs leaving a numbness that passed back down her arm toward the palm of her left hand and out of her fingertips. Lime colored sparks replaced them. Evy instantly thought at the sight of them, that they would scorch her flesh, leaving horrific scars in their places.

Page 60.

Nothing happened, Evy looked up for some sort of answer. Aiden's eyes were focused on her fingers. she was baffled, no answers to explain what was happening. Turning her gaze toward the mysterious man, who had a cool contempt about him. His gaze met her's the second she turned her face toward him. His smile even brighter than the last time Evy looked up at him. His jaw clenched in an untidy way. Opening his mouth to say..

"Thank you, sir Aiden McTavish. For bringing her here into my clutches. Here is your due for the young maiden." Then his grimy slime ridden hand pulled a large bag of coins from his dusty mite infested pocket. "You may leave her here, now be on your way. Shall our paths cross once more in a better time." Evy's hand went cold. she felt paralized, the last of his words amplified in slow motion. she never thought she would feel this way. frozen in time struck with numbness. Aiden had set her up. Evy had been betrayed by him which she thought she loved soo much. Evy's left hand that had flames. Turned to ice and shattered to a million peices as she clenched her fist to her chest. Evy released the grip of her right palm. Looking at Aiden. Watching him step back, after recieving the ruby red bag covered in dirt. Keeping his eyes downcast, his lips turned up to a sheepish grin.

Page 61.

He had sold her. Evy's face leeked ice tears that slid down her face to shatter in the dirt covered stone floor. Evy couldn't control her tears, as he left her in this unknown place.

"Do not fear, My dear. you are now my servant and you shall travel with me and my ship, The Equadorian Siren."

After his words were not responded toward. His Grin turned greedy stretching out his already marble colored face.

The door swung open with such haste. Evy's heart almost lept out of her chest. Turning away from her new nameless master.

Evy's eyes rested comfortably on the young girl standing in the arched doorway. Her hair long and black. Lips as red as a blushing rose. Eyes green as the vile ocean that they were about to embark onto.

Page 62.

Chapter Nineteen;
The Voyage To Emptyness.

The girl walked toward Evy, stopped and reached out to grasp her right palm. Leading Evy out and away from that dank room.

They Passed the stairs headed down a narrow hall lit only by candle light. Other than that, it was still pretty depressing and dark. The atmosphere gave off a eerie mellow feeling. Evy followed the beauty into the next room on their left, she followed close behind the girls swaying dress.. This room was slightly brighter than the last room they came from. Letting go of Evy's hand, the girl stoped in the center. Turning on her heals, the girl began to examine Evy for inspirational thought.

Page 63.

The girl began to undress Evy's pearl hair clips, releasing her auburn tresses to dangle freely down her creamy flesh back. Whilest the girl was in the moment of unclipping her hair. She had to reach up, brushing soft flesh and material together.

Their skin touched and the girls hair gave off a citris aroma that filled Evy's lungs. the girls mouth reached up to Evy's ear to whisper in such a melodic tone. her legs began to quiver and lose all meaning to gravity. Evy felt featherish. "My name is Gabriella, I know exactly who you are." Gabriella's warm honey flavored breathe rested comfortably on Evy's shoulder. her mind began to spin in all different directions. "Why am I here?" Was all Evy could get out, due to sheer panic. Gabriella's response was a mixture of undeniable comfort with a sense of fantastic unrealism to her sensitive ears. "You are the chosen one or so I've been told. A horrific battle's a bruin. Two men have been rivals since they were born. Torn from their mothers womb at the same time. Only royalty in Embala gives twins. These twins have pure hate for eachother. Although they don't look alike, they are a form of twin. Both evil in their own way. They also were obsessed with the myth our Eldor's passed down about a girl. You, Evy. Is all everyone chatts about. Since our

Page 64.

64

world shook to an Awakening state. Then news traveled about you being found uncouncious on the embankment. Both men will not yield or end the fued over your hand. They will keep coming after you. On either side of the war. The result is the same. Utter Chaos and distruction. People will die for you and that is why you are going into hiding with Olivander and the crew until we can figure how to dispell their advances."

"What of my brother?, What will I do without him. I need to find him and we must escape and go home." After saying what Evy's heart yearned to understand. The room turned cold and Gabriella pulled back. Eyes as cold as green ice. A harshness over came her. The tone of her voice soon changed in the same direction. "Your Brother isn't our concern. Be well aware that we, as in our world will put our problems in front of you. You will help us solve them before we tend to your selfishness." Gabriella then turned and grabbed a garmet out of an oak cedar chest. Placing it on the bed. After giving Evy the cold shoulder for atleast fifteen seconds. Gabriella Turned to face her then began undoing the wedding dress Evy was wearing Only to toss it violently into the darkest corner to a chair that was covered in dozens of cobwebs. While the material crushed through the ancient webs and landed on the redwood. Something moved in

Page 65.

the shadowed depth of the corner. The chair suddenly stood on it's hind
legs. Growling ferociously in a hungry snarl. The seat itself split in two
revealing rows of sharp teeth and a serpent tongue that lashed out around
the room. Then wiping the material from it's snout to suck it in like a toad.

The sight of something so grizzly stunned her. Evy's mouth lay gaped
open and her eyes frozen in place. Not knowing what just happened and
hoping that the incident wouldn't repeat itself.

Evy's fear lept into the future. To when some unsuspecting civilian
wanted to take a load off and sit on that chairs snout.

her thoughts were rudely disconsorted by a rude and disturbing
burp from the satisfied chair. Then returning to it's natural state.

Gabriella watched the magical monstrious chair, then returned her
gaze to Evy shocked pressence. Gabriella's eyes went from cold to warm
and sensitive. Moving behind Evy, Gabriella began to place the new
clothes on her. The mirror standing beside Evy, gave her some confidence.
Looking at Evy's new outfit a little bit satisfied by how normal she looked.
Evy was wearing a light blue maids outfit with a white apron that held her
dress tight against her curving body and hid her modest clevage. she truly
looked like a servant. When Evy was gazing at herself, she realized how

truly angry and hurt she felt over Aidens dishonorable acts of treachery. Her eyes began to swell with pain while her heart shattered in that instant. Gabriella reached her soft hands toward Evy's face cradling Evy's chin in her palms. "What is wrong, girl?" Asking in hushed tones. Evy Shook her head, glancing away from Gabriella's curious eyes. But Gabriella's sympathetic ocean colored eyes showed she cared. Evy's vision began to blur due to a wave of haziness and tears. The haziness held it's grip. Pulling her sleeve up to wipe away the dissapointment that seemed to linger on her face. "Nothing Gabriella, I just don't understand why my fingers began to spark, or the reason for this war that split the world." Gabriella turned and walked away through another door. Almost giving up on un-answered questions and finding the truth. Evy felt that Gabriella had abandoned her. Evy sat on the edge of the bed sulking in unwanted feelings. Sitting for a few seconds waiting. Gabriella suddenly appeared and told Evy to follow her. Evy skirted past the alarming chair. Following Gabriella through another door and down some spiral stairs out of the building. The night sky was royal blue with half a million dancing stars relaxing comfortably around a giant planet, The size of the moon, with a base converged underwater.

Page 67.

It was the most beautiful thing Evy's ever seen. Sparkling brighter than all the stars combined.

In front of her stood a dock made of cedar wood. Around the dock water enveloped everything. Dark and glimmering with small waves rippling with life. A minty aroma tickled Evy as the wind brought it against her skin. Behind Evy two lamps held up by gargoyle statues flickered. Giving Gabriella's figure a nice and creapy look. Pine tree's hiding in the distance, gave the land they were born on, a ruggid edge. Looking past Gabriella and over the dock from a distance. Evy noticed that the water moved from her left side to her right side. Evy saw that a nice and thick dirt brown rope sat comfortably around the post. Like a web of deciept, it slowly recoiled itself around the post a few more times and slunk over the splintered edge into emptyness like a lifeless slithering serpant. As they approached the rope, a sound caught Evy's attention. A sobbing creature filled the silence with whales of histarics. Everything went darker. Then out of habbit Evy decided against good judgement and turned. With no sense of light except the floating planet hanging behind her. A green figure at least ten feet tall stood before her stunned eyes. Evy looked it up and down. Unsure of her sanity, and if she was seeing, what she was seeing.

Page 68.

Still in disbelief as water dripped off the figure.

Gabriella ran quickly to the rope and began to untie the twisted slump. Looking briefly over Evy's shoulder toward Gabriella. "Evy, hurry. Amnark!" Unsure of herself, or of what she heard. Gabriella's words were slow and drawn out. Evy on the other hand couldn't move a muscle from her chest down. Evy's legs stiffened up and her feet were heavy. "Whats an Amnark?, Is this vile creature an Amnark?"

Evy said over, and over again, in a repetative way, to herself in her head, silently screaming. Evy felt as heavy as dirt packed tightly down in a bag or box. The Amnark budged. Shaking ferociously. Water lept free of the monster and skattered wet puddles all over Evy. Now her hair stuck to her face, Beginning to knott into tight curls. Teeth glinting red and eyes as black as desolate shimmering water, at night in the shadows. He stepped forward and put all his weight on his right foot. Standing less than a couple of feet away from Evy. Now towering her like a huge cedar tree. At his side, he had a battle ax. Covered in a multitude of ruby's, saphires, diamonds. With a gold etched line that wiggled a uniquely creepy design that sent chills up Evy's spine and made her blood tingle. The sharp ends of the ax was silver plated.

Page 69.

Shaking it a couple of times to air dry it. He lifted it up high above Evy. Then after reaching it's ultimate height, he began to bring it down with such force. her mind was racing with fear as everything went in slow motion again. The Ax glinted in the light from the water planet behind Evy. Looking into it's reflection to see Gabriella throwing the rope into the water and making her way toward Evy. She swears Gabriella's lips were saying the same panicked instructions over and over again. Inches from Evy's head she stuck the palms of her hands in the air in a deffensive task. Evy's hands got another numbing sensation, that spread through her body, protruding a forcefield. Still glancing at the ax, Evy's reflection appeared. her eyes, letting off a bright mixture of blue, lime, and lavender. her face was pale and unsure. The shield stretched around Evy and Gabriella. The monster brought down his weapon, to have it bounce off and send a shock of electric impulses through him. Something cautiously slithered secretively up on him. Letting a gleam give Evy warning. As a sword was thrust under his arm piercing the skin, releasing blood. The sword slid in as easy as a butterknife to butter. he fell effortlessly into the water. Sinking into the darkness. Before his head was fully submerged, he winked. Evy was taken back by his gesture. Fingers walked up the back of his head to the

Page 70.

top of it. A girl emerged out of the water resting her palm on his scalp. Skin pale blue and slimy. Fingers sucking onto his skin for a tight hold. The webbing glittered as her hair sopping wet, thick and tangled black. Just as her eyes were. Sea weeds clung to her like a magnet. She looked up at Evy and grinned shards of teeth, at least three rows that pushed out as she let out a scream of hunger and impatience. Her fingers tightened as she drug him fully under. Bubbles of a fight rippled to the surface. Then Nothing. Evy was left there, gaping into the black hell from underneath them.

A couple of hands grasped Evy from around her wrists, to bring them down to her sides. Looking back to where the Amnark used to be standing. Dazed Evy said the creatures discripted name aloud. "Amnark?" In it's place a woman stood. Her hair long and brown with some highlights that glinted from the planets light. Her eyes were pure white. She stood there for a moment examining Evy like a unique new shiny toy. "Hello Evy, you sure are something special. I've heard the rumors were true, but as I hold your wrists. I can't help but see into your past, present, and future. You sure are something more than Extraordinary." Evy's mouth dropped to a frown then. "Everyone keeps telling me this. But

"I'm only here for my brother. And if I must go through your hell to get him, then I will do what I have to. To get him back."

The womans smile got even larger at Evy's last spoken words.

"Ah.... I see you are on a grand quest full of many dangerious tasks to find your twin brother Ashton."

The whole time Evy was here, she never once told this woman or anyone that information.

"how did you know he was my twin?"

Eyes twinkling.

"The same way I know that you were to be betrothed, to sir Henry Lockhart."

"Huh?"

"For someone special you seem a little thick under your scalp, I'm a Cleravoint, The one they call Fortuna. But you Evy Trinity Bridgewater can call me Lucinda Barthalemew or simply my friends call me Luci, I hope soon you will become an ally and a friend."

"Nice to meet you Fortuna......er...Miss Barthalemew.....Um, sorry I mean Luci." Smiling Evy raised her hand politely and shook Luci's.

"Ah hemm.'Gabriella caughed.

Page 72.

"Hurry up Luci, and Evy. Before another vile water creatain or Amnark comes after us again."

With a large sigh, they followed Gabriella, to a most unusual sailor. The whole boat was darkly painted and glimmering like the water underneath it. A lage post stood up at the tip, and there was a strange small hunched wolf gargoyle bowing with his tongue out and rippling like a wave with a stone. That reflected the same color that came from Evy when she would do strange stuff.

Page 73.

The Title of A Crucified Innocence.

Chapter Twenty;

Waking Up On A Bed Of Water.

Evy cracked her eye lids to the dim light, and it wasn't easy.
Especially when it was coming through the cyllinder window above the
canopy. Raising herself was tricky as well, when the bed she was in, was
made up of a knetted sheet hooked up on opposite walls stretching out. Evy
pulled the thin blanket off of herself and raised her legs up, to bring them
over the edge. While she was trying not to flip out of bed and land on her
face. she began to sit up. The smell of pine wood lingered in the
atmosphere. Evy figured the smell was coming from the log walls. The
cabin was but a small chamber or cell. Across from her, a cedar chest
was cracked open. Hopping off of the bed, Evy decided to make her

Page 74.

way across the room to investigate it. Tip toeing over the cool floorboards.

Evy's mind filled with curiosity. Looking over the edge of it's walls. A sheet of partchment lay tame and delicate. In black ink etched in the white paper read....

"Dearest Evy;

For you.

xoxoxo

P.S. come see the Captn'

when Ready Fin." What? Setting the paper aside, Evy noticed a bundle of clothes were packed with a shiny pair of black boots. Thinking they must be for her, Evy began to undress the white apron and make her way through the blue dress. Dropping them on the cool maple floor boards. she turned back to the chest to pull out a pair of stockings, some black trousers and a white blouse with a black vest. The only three remaining items left in the chest were a lavender ribbon to tie back Evy's auburn curls. The black boots and a sword wrapped in a black sash. looking at herself and at how amazing she looked. Remembering the stories of famous pirates that made her smile. An adventurious journey she will go on for her brother and this world. They were both fortunate Evy was

Page 75.

here in their survival through the gruesome battles learking upon them in the dark shadows of Life.

Page 76.

Chapter Twenty One;
　　　Lost But Not Found

Ahckmelutra paced the room after his angry roar toward Evy's escape into The Truscan Forest. He almost had her. Showed her such compassion. What could have went wrong? The rain started to pour in heavy sheets as he thought back to her folly decision. His thoughts were rudely disconsorted by rain heavily thudding against the castle walls.

Out of the corner of his eye, a shadow moved. Turning his eyes upward. His Generals gaze met his.

(General Aiden McTavish)

"I want you to find her and bring her back to me."

His demand was met with a gentle yet stern

Page 77.

understanding of the stakes.

"Yes, Messiah Ahckmelutra."

Some sort of contorted certanty mixed with a mask of seriousness crossed over Aiden's face. You could tell that his emerald eyes couldn't hold a secret locked away in a treasured volt. But his lips straightened into a hard line and he left before Ahckmelutra had a chance to blink in all the misfortune his day had taken.

Certain he was alone. Ahchmelutra began to turn back toward the window to pound both his clenched fists on the seil. Making emense splashes that lifted into the air at impact and soaked his face.

Drenching all of his slicked back silky hair into his eyes. Covering his menacing expression of hurt and hate.

Setting his head down on his hands in frustration for a moment then pulling his head up with all his might to growl into the night sky as thunder met his sadistic cry into the heavens. his hair completely soaked flew back as his head rushed up and rested in a sopping pile behind his scalp. Rain turning into moistened steam as the thunder and his growl shook the heavy curtains of clouds making them ripple in a most undesirable way. Changing into the very creature he hates.....A Lycan!

Page 78.

Chapter Twenty Two;
Looking For Unexpected Love.

The black stallion trodded heavily across the sopping gravel, making splashes every few moments. Heart beating heavy and muscles stretching tensly. Beads of sweat and water trailed endlessly off of the moving creatures magnanimious limbs. Nostrils flamed as it's steams continues to eat into the misty early morning atmosphere. Where suddenly the speed took a new turn. The light of day was starting to break through the clearing. Tree's and mountains stood tall up ahead. Water started to get lighter and less frequent as everything began to dry in the hasty light of Embala's sun's

Page 79.

A town called Shreve Grove, hid around the bin curve of the trail. A place considered sacred, giving off a warm sensation of safety. The town of Shreve Grove wasn't easily found as the founding fathers put a safety curse on it so no one except the towns people or the propherical girl could find it and be safe.

A nice place to rest for a short while and refresh Ithica. Hopping off of her, Aiden patted Ithica on the side of her head. Taking the reins to a near by post. The stable boy named Will, pulled up some hay and a bowl of refreshing water. Will was a good boy who tended to Aiden's horse more than a few dozen times. Letting the small toe head boy keep her company until it was time to leave. Aiden stood there rubbing Ithica's head, thinking back to a few short hours ago at the castle. To when he saw Evy running toward him. Near the west wall of The Truscan Forest. Her Auburn hair flailing violently and full of passion against the wind. Her green eyes glimmering in hope and desperation as her legs thrust her foreward knocking soft warm flesh into him accidently. Aiden even remembered her lavender scented skin. How could he not forget her. Angelicaly gracefull as she got up from him and began gathering her few yet simple possessions to leave him.

Page 80.

Aiden wanted to hold on to her and never let go. When he tried then she resisted his embrace. It only made him want her even more. Body and soul.

She kicked him hard knocking him back on his butt. Aiden Rushed to his feet trying to stop her fall backward down that steep hill. Hitting every branch to the bottom of the trench. Watching the black abyss swollow her whole as her eyes filled with distress. It was like a dream. Grogginess of witnessing something so unbelievable. Aiden thought he was day dreaming. It seemed unreal. Unsure of what just happened. maybe it was a really great fantasy. Snapping out of it, Aiden looked up toward the castle and at his king, who growled heavily into absolete ignorant wind. Aiden knew then, that something was urgently wrong. Rushing up to his kings aid he found out, what he knew was certain. Aiden must find and retrieve Evy. An ache rippled from his beating heart for the girl and her misfortune to come. Death, Greed, Destruction and Futile Discruptincy of love for her. Touching and seeing her, he knew she was the one he must rush toward safety. Mind returning to present, Aiden moved to Will and patted his favorite nephew to say. "Good Job laddy." Aiden, then proceeded toward The Towering Twins Inn. The door was ajar. As he knocked a bit, then walked right in.

The first sight he saw was the beautiful Mary Elizabeth Shaw.

A rotundant woman whom he loved and adored since she was a wee baby in her nursery. As his mother fed her and sung her Lullibies of long told prophecy as nursing rhymes.

His sister and her husband owned The Towering Twins Inn. Mary had long brown hair tied back in a braided knotted bun ontop of her crown. Tresses fell everywhere as she looked up from the floor and was astonished to find her brother standing before her.

Aiden watched as Mary Elizabeth glanced up with a glimmering smile. Her hands were red from all the excessive scrubbing and her face was sullied from all the sweat pouring down her brows.

His smile helped lift her spirit as she raised herself up from the floor and gave him a friendly warm hug. Her on her knee's and him half on his.

They held eachother for a few minutes until her husband Gregory Thomas Shaw entered the room. He was stunned at how they held eachother in a half embrace. "Mary, dearest. Give the man a break, He's been riding all morning long. He need's a good meal in him."

"Oh. Yes, Gregory. You are sure right."

"Come Aiden, let's get you fed before you get

Page 82.

any skinnier."

With that he shook his head.

"I cannot stay long, I am pursuing the kings new bride, The one from the prophecy. She has lept out of the highest tower and now is on foot in The Truscan Forest."

"Oh my goodness, Aiden. Hope has come at last. When you find her, can we see her?" "I'm sorry to dash your hopes Mary Elizabeth. But the king wants her immediatly. So I cannot offord any rest stops or mistakes. As you may recall the circumstances of the last General. Who's place I took. They beheaded him for sleeping in too late, due to strong mead and three of the shepards daughters in his bed chambers." Gregory added with a stern face "Sire Ahckmelutra was furious!" Her eyes already appoligizing before her lips. "Oh, I'm deeply sorry for asking." Gregory chipped in another shilling of words. "My wife is so prudent in childish things. I guess thats why I married her. Love wasn't an option." They all laughed Mary Elizabeth left with a frown and anger rising in her icy blue eyes. She set her consintration on working on breakfast for her older brother. While her husband mingled with him on prior events. After gobbling down all the food, and finishing

Page 83.

news of old times. Aiden was ready to say goodbye and head out.

His sister's eye's were a little sad but she knew dropping a few tears would do no good at keeping him there.

Ithica was half asleep and bored out of her mind, waiting for Aiden to untie her. He Said..

"Farewell for now little Will, take care of your parents for me."

"Okay, best of Luck on your quest for the escaped bride."

He left the small village of Shreve Grove to continue the quest. Riding out of Shreve Grove was peaceful. All the villagers were still in slumber. The sun's warmth sat gently on Aiden's shoulders. Warm weather spread across the country side and slumbering peasants. Everything seemed to come to life. Colors etched the hills and forest around him.

Heading toward the west wall of The Truscan Forest. He began to scan around to find the spot she might've fallen.

A couple of minutes later, he finally found what he was looking for. Broken branches down the steep hill side. And a rock, sharp and pointy with dried crusts of blood on it. Taking in his surroundings. He saw a trail of broken twigs heading west/east and followed. She must've been close, because the footprints were warm.

Page 84.

Following them for about ten minutes on horseback. A sound startled Ithica and rang in Aidens ears. A horse drawn carriage Moving fast up ahead. A little further he spotted her. Stock still like a deer in fright. Fearing for her life. Not waisting a seconds hesitation. Kicking Ithica into a fast sprint. A minutes too late would have killed her. But he was an expert at saving dansil's in distress. Picking her up like picking up dasy's in the woods and setting her down on the back of Ithica. Aiden got his wish. Her arms warm and slender held on to him and he was relishing in this monumental moment, that he wouldn't take for granted. They continued to head west/east trotting fast. Then when Aiden thought they would be safe. he stopped at skeleton waterfall peak. Where rushing water cascaded out of the rock shaped like a skull. He remembered partial stories about it. That the skull itself was a demi god named Nemosi. Who died in a battle while protecting all of Embala millions of years ago from a supernatural being that could hide as smoke and overpower it's enemy and kill. While squeezing the life force out of them from within. Thinking back to the story. A huge factorial or historical chunk was missing. That his ancestors had long forgotten. Staring at it now gave Aiden uncontrolable waves of rippling goosebumps. Ithica slowed to a walking pace, Aiden gracefully hopped off of her and returned to help Evy off of his steed. Looking at Evy now, he could tell how shooken up she was. Her hands were shaking uncontrolably. A sudden contradiction to her eyes that showed no fear, only thanks from a good strong heart. He also noticed that she was curious to who her masked rescuer was. So in that instant he threw off his hooded attire and greeted her. Before he could get a word out, she was flushing with embarrassment. Her cheeks almost matched her flaming hair. He couldn't remember what was all said, but he did remember how she didn't recognize him. How she must've lost her memory of who she was. So he decided to leave her to build camp. Leaving to find a member of the order to consult these issues with. He left Ithica with Evy and walked deeper and deeper into The Death Forest. The further he went in. Death reaked through out the air. Wind kicked up and chidded roughly past his already chapped cheeks. Good thing his beard was growing. Not a big help but it did have it's benefits. Although the wind did leave a stinging sensation that kept him alert for oncoming prey in this part of the dreary forest. Hunting always came easy to him since childhood. Aiden figured he could catch something warm and edible for both their aching stomaches. Walking began to take it's toll on him. After hours of riding to find her. He knew time was wearing him out.

The sun's began to come closer to setting and he needed to hurry. A dark cottage sat behind some pretty solid leaves. Vines drenched over it. Hiding from all the world to find it. Walking around it to the entrance. Then pulling the hanging leaves out of the way and to the side.

He entered complete darkness. Steep stairs descending. With little light eluminating the passageway. At the bottom he met Olivander the head of the secret salvation of the world of embala.

Or as he liked to call it (The Sso Twoe)

Eyes were shining in the dark as he met his unexpected guest.

"Hello General Aiden McTavish, what brings you here on such short notice?" Aiden Answered. "She has arrived and the Sire of Embala wish's to marry her, but first he sends me on a quest to find her. Since she escaped like a pro out of his highest tower." Now Olivander's eyes closed and his mouth gaped open like a serpant. With shards of unhuman teeth that pushed into an utmost unpleasant smile.

"Ah, I felt her when she arrived. At first I thought the ground beneath our feet were rumbling a seriously dangerious warning. Altering a cataclismic Events."

Page 87.

"Oh, yes. I felt it too."

Aiden added. Olivander lifted his hand in the darkness and shifted to his left side. With his long nailed, webbed fingers he moved them up and down beckoning the cauldrin to come to his call. It lifted up from the ground and floated around him to sit in the center between him and Aiden.

The icy flames flickered to life around the cyllinderic ball in the center. Lime sparks moved behind leaving the air crisp and fresh. "Do you know the myth of the foretold skull waterfall?"

Aiden took another gulp of crisp air and added.. "We've all heard rumors, but I cannot recall the entire story from memory. Only bit's and pieces." Olivander brought his hand around and patted it down to set the cauldrin down. As he did that. Two chairs skimmed the floor barely touching their weight to the cold icy dirt covered concrete. Knocking Aiden off his feet onto the chair unexpectadly. Olivander floated upward and folded his legs in a back hop onto the chair. After sitting for a few seconds. Olivander pulled his hand out of his pocket to reveal blue sparkling dust that he flecked into the cauldrin. "Along time ago a war raged between two demi-god men. One for the better and the other for the worst. Both sexually infatuated with the same women. But she only loved one. Now mind you these men

Page 88.

were on the borderline of psychologically dangerious. Sounds familiar? Well the women fell in love. But the love of her man was threatened, so she gave herself up to marry the other. On their wedding night he murdered her because he felt if he could not conqure all of her then no one could have her. You see her body and soul belonged to Nemosi. But she never once yielded her heart to the one who tricked her. Stockrows was the other man, he was cruel. Stockrows was part god, he could control fire and smoke while Nemosi was able to control earthly elements such as water and land."Continues... "Nemosi was furious with heart ache and vengence carved a place in his soul filling every fragment of his being with hate. They each yielded a sword and faught ferociously, splitting hair's. In a grip they held until each of them at the same time pulled out the daggers that were forged together at their birth. Poison infected both body's turning them into vicious animals. Then dieing slowly together with daggers ripping a splurge of blood that dripped until no life remained. Nemosi rests on his stomach always crying. Nose, eyes, mouth turned to waterfalls. The other.... stockrows on his back where he turned to smoke, slowly dissintigrating all that remains of the sorrow and betrayal is Nemosi's skull. Skull Waterfall."

Page 89.

After telling Aiden this, he began to understand similar events will occure and history will indeed repeat itself. Watching the magic dust dissintigrate into the skin of the ball of flames.

The center turned warm and he noticed that the ball was giving off a warm light.

The image was Evy. He saw that she was in trouble. He lept for the door but before he could completely reach it. Olivander called to him. Looking back the thin man tossed him a large bag of good luck dust to ensure he can get out of any jam.

Page 90.

Chapter Twenty Three;
Frantic Rescue

Rushing himself up the spiral staircase was nothing but urgent in the matter of Evy. At the top of the stairs he lunged himself out the open weed door. Flailing his sword like a wild man in love.

Heart beating fast and weary. Billowing clouds began to throw sheets of ice down on him. Preventing his speed to hasten.

For every ten steps forward, he was thrust backward five. Ice literally began burning his warm skin with sharp tips. The wind kicked in to assist the harsh weather. Up ahead out of the darkness a light reflected off of the tent illuminating the surrounding brush.

A shadow flickered through the tent. From the

Page 91.

curves of it, he could tell it was Evy.

Finally the wind died down and the shards became soft and fell like dust in slow motion. The shadow inside began to struggle and panic against invading arms.

Aiden decided to skirt around the tent, in hopes of catching the perpatraitor by surprise. Almost to the entrance and..

"Bang!!"

His head spinning from the contact of whatever struck him silently. Silent echoe's repeadedly conquired his mind as he fell forward onto the snow, landing on his side.

Eyes becoming blurry as he watched helplessly as two men carried Evy to the cart and loaded her into the cage. Eyes flickering backwards into Aiden's head until the world fell silent around him.

Page 92.

Chapter Twenty Four;
The Hunt.

Waking up was irritating to Aiden. He was both cold and warm as he opened his eyes. Expecting the unexpected. White surrounded him. He began to wiggle around to shake off the pile of powder snow that had begun to harden into rock.

Standing was a bit of a daze as he recalled the prior events of the evening before looking a bit on the shaky side at the camp Evy had built for them. The tent torched and in a pile of crispy ashes ingulfed in a wreckage of snow. His horse Ithica was no where to be seen. He turned to skull waterfall and began to climb

Page 93.

it. Both of Embala's sun's were up and doing a great job at melting the snow quickly.

At the top he stood looking out over his surroundings. Tree's shook the snow from their branches, literally flickering them. Before his eyes, the snow had melted any trace of them being there.

Rushing the little puddles that seeped from the grass and gravel into the exotic river. It was utterly amazing. The wind warm and friendly brushed pass Aidens sullen face.

Pulling out the bag Olivander had given him. It looked like the color of ruby blood contaminated with dirt. Grasping a bunch of white and silver dust in his right hand. He tossed it up into the air and expertly yanked his sword out and slashed a pattern into the floating dust.

Left, Right. Up, Down. Tossing it up into the air and expertly yanked his sword back in it's fold of the diced substance.

Stashing his sword back in it's fold of the hilt, To watch the dust do it's magic.

Chapter Twenty Five;
Journey To Desirable Emptyness.

The dust stretched and contorted itself at unbearable lengths. The mirror image stretched out like a silver silky bedsheet. Reflecting small shards flickering through an eminant space.

Dozens upon dozens, floating about like empty square bubbles. One flickered through the rest. Cutting into each of them. Leaving bite marks. Spinning fast setting off splintering waves, rippling off of the edge. Stretching to fit the cyllinderic mirror. The image was unfocused. Slowly defragmenting towards clearity. Evy lay curled up in the fetal position. Her skin blue as ice and cold to the touch. Her breathing a little unregular. Hair red as auburn leaves on fire and

Page 95.

disconsorted. Webs of tangled strands lay comfortably over her tender soft face covering bits of it. A moan left her lips but soon diminished into desirable emptyness

The image pulled out and focused on her surroundings. In a box. Zooming further outward. A cage wrapped in animal skins on the back of a creaky red wood built wagon.

On a road headed toward The Dark Castle of Sire Showknizar.

"Sire Iolis."

left his lips briefly while stepping off of the tip of the skull, like walking on an invisible force. Falling in a slowish motion. Robe flailing against the savage wind. He landed with his left knee hugging the ground and his right in the position for a proposal. His left palm eating into the soft gravel and his head bent. He whistled, Ithica came rushing to her masters side prancing to a slowing pace behind him. Still on the ground waiting for the opertune moment to fling into a backflip and a mix of a horizontal and vertical side flip onto the back of Ithica's saddle. Resting comfortably on her for a moment longer, nudging her into a sprinting dash headed into the thicker, colder brush of the dark forest. Chills rippling off of Ithica's black coated skin, leaving icy cold sweat pouring into empty stale air.

Page 96.

Chapter Twenty Six;
        Devious Conversations.

The castle and it's walls up ahead were burnt black. That color to show as one would think that the Empire inside wasn't as friendly. Heaps of billowing thunderious clouds covered the sky. The woods surrounding the castle were a darkening shadow. The bridge up ahead was an old cracking mess that wood worms feasted upon all the time. Trotting galliently up to the entrance, Caution vibed around Aiden's frazzled nerves. Darkness approached like a cotton blanket softly covering all of Embala. The torches on each side of the drawbridge gate were lit and gleaming. Leaving a hazy warm glow stretching around the entrance lighting the way

Page 97.

to the inside. Sliding off of Ithica with great gentility.

"Who goes there!"

A soldier stepped out of the curtains of tree's. His heals eating into the gravel. This man was entirely covered in dark auburn coat of fur. From head to toe. From his waist down he was in Sire Polls's guard uniforms. Holding a torch, Stepping closer to Aiden he asks again.

"Who goes there!"

Voice humming a vivacious growl. Aiden knew there weren't going to be anymore chances for this guard to ask again.

"Reloes, you old dog. Tis Aiden McTavish."

The snout of Reloes twitched into an upright smile.

"Aiden, where have you been."

Aiden stepped forward reaching his right hand out to except Reloes's grasp. In a friendly manner.

"Reloes, I have taken some time to visit my deathly ill family."

"I'm sorry to hear that. my best reguards. I do hope your family recovers from the travesty." "Granted, I'm pleased that you are a great soldier and friend. That I'm able to comand in any situation." "Thank you, General. Have you heard the grand news?"

Page 98.

to the inside. Sliding off of Ithica with great gentility.

"Who goes there!"

A soldier stepped out of the curtains of tree's. His heals eating into the gravel. This man was entirely covered in dark auburn coat of fur. From head to toe. From his waist down he was in Sire Iolis's guard uniforms. Holding a torch, Stepping closer to Aiden he asks again.

"Who goes there!"

Voice humming a vivacious growl. Aiden knew there weren't going to be anymore chances for this guard to ask again.

"Reloes, you old dog. Tis Aiden McTavish."

The snout of Reloes twitched into an upright smile.

"Aiden, where have you been."

Aiden stepped forward reaching his right hand out to except Reloes's grasp. In a friendly manner.

"Reloes, I have taken some time to visit my deathly ill family."

"I'm sorry to hear that. my best reguards. I do hope your family recovers from the travesty." "Granted, I'm pleased that you are a great soldier and friend. That I'm able to comand in any situation." "Thank you, General. Have you heard the grand news?"

Page 98.

Water splashing under the def echo of the bolt. A subsided struggle that ended quickly and jingling keys in a lock. Focusing back on Reloes, Aiden began to say... "I have to take Ithica to the stables and head to my chambers for a quick change, do you mind if I go? Although our chat was quite extraordinary, I'm weary and am in need of a quick rest before I present myself to our beloved Sire Iolis." "Tis not a problem dear comrad, I will see you at the dinner celebration after the wedding." With that reloes shook the rain off like a wet wild animal and fur sprouted. Covering his skin instantly. Turning toward Ithica, Aiden grasped her reins tightly and guided her across the bridge. At the other end, he turned to Reloes and waved. Reloes yelled out... "Get feeling better, I think exhaustion is making you repeat yourself." Aiden watched as Reloes turned with his torch of light and stepped behind the curtain of forest and misty rain. fog alooped the outer area of the forest. Going through the arched gate, Aiden whispered a coded comand to Ithica. Ithica turned and headed for food, water and shelter. After watching her leave. Aiden turned to a brick in the wall's surface. Pulling out his bag of dust. He tossed a handfull of the sparkly substance on the wall, watching it shatter on the bricks.

Pushing the rough surface deeper inside the wall.

Page 100.

Unclenching and releasing a passageway.

The Title Of A Crucified Innocence

Chapter Twenty Seven,
Flames Of Passionate Jealousy

Aiden tried to pre-pare himself for what he might see and the emotion he is bound to feel. Sneaking through the tunnels was easy. Down there all he had to sneak past, were sewer rats and they weren't always a huge concern. But she was. Sliding up the ladder like a slithering serpant to enter through the security hatch. To the most used room in the castle, The Kitchen. That was the tricky part. Hustle and bustle was all he could hear from loud and obnoxious servants and cooks as they frantically rushed to pull off the unevitable. Good thing a large cabinet and barrels of liquare blocked anyone's view. Giving enough cover for him to

Page 102.

move fast and silently. The kitchen was always a rough obstacle. Crouching low against the barrels. Pulling out a small round shaving mirror to stratagize a plan to leave the kitchen. Doing the crabwalk, he crept close to the edge and looked out. No way out. The crabwalk was not the most easiest skill to aquire, but Aiden pulled it off. To his right stood an open archway. All he had to do is get there undetected. The area he was held up in, was lit by a candle on the table above the secret door. It danced to the current of air. Right then and there Aiden knew what he needed to do. Hand full of silver dust he blew a gust of his magic toward the lonesome candle flame. Extinguishing it's warmth and serenity. Pitch darkness filled all the dimentional crevices in the small space. Giving a welcoming cover to Aiden as he did a side roll across the stone floor and out of the kitchen. Thinking he was safe, was an understatement as he stood and was nearly trampled by a aggrivated servant carrying a huge white wedding cake. Luckily he moved fast enough to get a cynnically angry glare from the servant. Now out of the hazerdious zone, he brushed the dirt off of him and looked around for her. Finding her with his eyes, he realized he needed better cover. A pillar a couple of feet from The Tenarion Throne of black shimmering steel. He

Page 103.

waited patiently and watched in complete silence only inches from being recognized by the king. Heart beating only for her. Seeing Evy. Sent rippled unnerving passion splintering through his veins, watching her blind fold slowly fall to the floor.

Eye's blinded by the sun's pressing through the glass arched windows. Aiden never knew a woman could have such an effect on him. Evy was shoved forward through the door frame into the great hall. Arms bound as she glided slowly down the row, shoulders slumped as if she were walking down death row. Her eyes wild but tame and harmless filled full of confussion. Seeing her treated in a barbaric way, enflamed rage in Aiden's eyes and twisted anger in his heart towards those damn vile Padowah. Not realizing his hands slide down the pillar edges to his dagger and thrashian rappier. She was barefoot, her dress ripped and filthy clinging to her warm moist skin. Barely hanging on her body. One could barely distinguish most of her bruises from blotches of dirt. Evy's hair was tangled and passionatly wild as if she were an avenging war angel. When the light of Embala's sun's kissed her hair and form. Crimson flames erupted, making her a most prized angelical spectacle. Only further proving the myths were acurate. As she reached Iolis. Aiden felt a gust of wind

Page 104.

move pass him. It was Sophie rushing away to do the king's bidding. He didn't pay attention to what the king was saying to her. Just the Possessive kiss and aggressive toss of her like a piece of cloth. Anger and jealousy flushed through Aidens veins showing flames in his eyes.

After the Padowah carried her off, Aiden followed behind. Like a fly on a wall. Stopping across the hallway. Evy was placed in the chamber across from his.

Walking up to his door as casual as possible glancing at the two guards.

"Gary and Larmain."

They nodded in unicen.

"Greetings General."

Then he stepped into his bed chamber and began to get clean and ready for his welcoming back Audience with Sire Iolis.

Chapter Twenty Eight;
Jealous Shell With No Soul.

Aiden entered Iolis's chambers in full uniform where he finds his king sitting in full view on the edge of his bed. Preparing for his wedding. "Always a pleasure to smell fresh and feel clean on a wonderful night like this one. Smiling up at Aiden as he spoke "Yes it is. I thought you yourself, would like to hear that I'm back from my home. Everything is going well." In a stern yet unsurprising tone. Iolis added. "General Aiden Mctavish, I would like to personally welcome you back." Pacing a bit then kneeling infront of Iolis.

Page 106.

"Congratulations M'Lord on getting married."

Iolis jumped up onto his feet and patted his hands devilishly and greedily together in a jesture of excitement.

"Tis a blessing from the god's."

Then turning away from the fireplace toward Aiden.

"You General, must go rest until the celebration."

Leaving, Aiden felt comforted relief. Walking back to his room, he brought Gary and Larmain some goblets of celebratory wine. Thanking him as he went into his room. Satisfied that no one knew he was up to no good.

In his room stood a bed with black silky sheets. Fluffed white cotten and cocoa colored wood. His bed glissening him to rest. In his heart he felt it wasn't time for that yet. At the end of the bed stood a wall fireplace with white and black tile and a mantle that was also white. In the right corner stood the mirror that reflected his harsh couple of days. Eyes going from emerald to piercing blue. Aiden lifted both eye brow's as he checked the bags under his eyes. Hair wavy and touching the middle of his neck. Not curly just glistening dark waves barely softly grazing his arched brow's. He enjoyed the new look. Stubbled beard, not dark as one would think, but light and gentle. He

Page 107.

imagined kissing Evy. Her fingers gliding through his hair and sliding down his cheekbone to carress his silky beard. Gliding down and around to where she clasped onto his neck and kissed him deeply. Kissing her would be a blessing and a curse to both their sacred lives. He hoped that she wasn't a dream. He couldn't bare the thought of waking up one morning and her existence was just a fictious fantasy. If this passion he felt for her were to remain but she weren't. He didn't think he could handle heartache. without her he felt he would cease to nothing more than an empty shell of dispair. He yearned her. Unable to bare it anymore he slid on his hooded cape and walked to the left side of the bed where a bookshelf was etched into the wall. A gargoyle statue hung on each side of the book case. Hunched in a growl position. Mouths snarling a glass ball of liquide flames. Taking both hands and stretching to lightly push the hornes into the scalps of the gargoyles releasing a latch. Both glass balls turning from yellow to blue as the shelf opened up to reveal a set of crued steps. Walking down under the hallway Gary and Larmain were stationed. But five feet across to another set of steps going up to Evy's room. Standing and waiting and watching helplessly was the hardest thing Aiden had to do in his entire life. Or so he thought. There she stood infront of the mirror. Looking

Page 108.

lavish in white. From his position he couldn't hear any of the conversation in her chamber. She stood there saying something to Sophie and it had the wrong effect. Next to Sophie stood Iolis. Face shocked and distraught as he ordered Sophie out and paced the room. Evy's face twisting to an appoligetic expression then she turned back to the mirror. Eyes down cast. Then Iolis was instantly behind her. His fingers and palm wrapped around the nape of her neck as he held her tall. Her weight lifting off of the ground. Feet barely able to braze the stool. He whispered harshly into her ear like a slithering serpant. Tears began to purge violently and emotionally down her cheeks and dampen part of her bussoms and gown. Something odd happened. Iolis glanced at her face in the mirror. His face twisting to regret as he let go and sprints out of the room. Guards locking the latch behind him. Silently she rubbed away tears that Aiden felt he should have handled for her. Sadness filled the spaces around her. Evaperating and his heart ached for her. Heart heeving wearily. She walked over to the seil of the window and held onto the wall for support as she slid down the sturdiest wall she could collapse in tears onto. her moans of distress were too much for Aiden's heart to handle. Aiden quietly skirted the edge of the book shelf.

Page 109.

In a transe he knew he wanted to be the one to make all her troubles go away and tell her it was all going to be alright.

Aiden found was standing over her. Taking her under her arms and holding her waist pulling her up to him. Her eyes down cast. Slowly rising up his body. then her green eyes glittered as our eyes met. Making Aidens heart slowed to skip a beat. A smile crept up her lips. She gave Aiden courage in that meraculious smile.

Aiden rested his palm on her rosy cheeks and gently wiped away her fears. Aiden wrapped his hand into her's. their fingers intertwined. Guiding her toward the book case in the wall. Sounds of feet shuffling outside. Aiden brought her around and pressed her against it. Arms held above her head. Kissing her in a gentle yet passionate way. De Ja Vu was all he could think. Sounds their hearts made were like horses thundering in a pack. Aiden felt like he was apart of her. He belonged with and too her. More clutter outside the room. Time to go. Aiden opened the book case and down they went. Light slowly drowning in darkness as the wall slid back into place behind them. Later outside, Aiden placed her on Ithica. While she was drowsy, he pulled out his Styth. An elemental charm that placed all objects into silent pause.

Page 110.

Aiden grabbed onto Ithica and Evy then spun it.

A huge pulse rivited through them making all time stop. Then Aiden slid infront of Evy and led the way to the Citadel of Olivander.

After riding back to the cottege covered in weeds, something seemed a tad bit odd. Aiden felt like someone or something was following them.

On top of the Citadel a crow sat feathers black and shimmering. But the crow itself wasn't odd. What did make him nausious was that a tiny fly sat on the crows back. As if it were riding it like a horse.

Page 111.

Chapter Twenty Nine;

Honerable Disheveled Secrets.

Aiden steps from out of the cabin room and takes the bag of coins and drops them into Gabriella's soft milky white fingers. Whispering in her ear. "Take care to conceal her identity and safety, When she is ready. Tell her the truth." Noticing this time the fly sat on the wall as if spying. But it couldn't be. Thats not even possible. Brushing it off as nothing but paranoia. He left out of the concealed cabin or as Olivander loved to call it, The Secret Citadel. All it was, was a fortress underground hidden as a cabin with jungle fever. Rushing as fast as the wind will let him go.

Page 112.

Ithica's hooves ate into the earth. Passing over the little bridge and into the arch way.

Hopping off of her. Ithica knew where the stables were and took herself.

Crossing into the Labrynth. All he encountered down below was a blur. Entering up his stairs into his bed chamber's. Making sure the gargoyles on his wall's glasses turned back to yellow flames.

He almost forgot about his Styth activation. But first he washed the dirt and filth off of him and rechanged.

Finally ready, he twitched the Styth and another vibrant shock rippled all around making everyone come to life.

With everything, he left for the great celebration telling Gary and Larmain that he would see them at the Ceremony. They smiled and continued chatting about Ancient long ago wars.

Page 113.

Chapter Thirty;
    Taken By Surprise.

        Iolis returned to his room to finish getting fitted. All in
black. No shirt and a jacketed robe gliding across the floor as he stood.
Black balloon shaped drawers. Metallic sabor and rappier slid between
the folds of cloth and his light tan sides.
        "Enter Sophie."
        He said before she had the luxery of knocking, He knew she
couldn't speak. but she told him in sign language that she was finished.
                Time Slows To A Pause

        Two large snakes slither off of the bed post. Wiggling as they take
human form. Both in loins cloth. One with hawk eye's and long black shiny
blue   Page 114.

tinted hair, hanging down his spine. The other with black eyes with sparks of red shooting out of the center. His hair short atleast to shoulder length. Hair black with sparks of red also shooting from the roots to the tips. both have skin soft and dark as worked leather.

"Lyco's, something strange has happened."

The younger one with red streaks says..

"Delvoir, someone has frozen time so they may escape unnoticed."

lycos shifts and morphs into a glistening crow while Delvoir turnes into a fly.

Black body, white wings with red lines shooting from the base. Lycos fly's to the window and turns to Delvoir.

"Hop on, so we might investigate." Delvoir glides through the room and lands on Lycos's back. then they take flight. Below the window they see a man and woman on horseback. Putting distance between The Dark Castle and them. The man was hard to see. His hood covered his Identity. Delvoir says..."Lycos, they're headed to The Death Forest where Olivander's Citadel is." A moments pause. "Fly fast to pass them so we can blend into the scenery." They sat there as uncanny as possible. After they went in. Lycos and Delvoir tried to get in. The

Page 115.

115

fly was easy to get in. But the crow went around, back to sit and wait on top of the tower. Lycos told Delvoir.

"If he comes out, follow him. I'm sure he's from the king's staff. Go now. If he does return. Be back in the room to report to master. If they leave, I'll communicate through telepathy."

Delvoir did what he said. Then high tailed it back to his masters chambers. He turned back into a snake and waited.

Time Slithers Into Play

Iolis sends a guard to tell Gary and Larmain to bring Evy. Soon after leaving. The guard returns with the two soldiers. Both men's faces were as pale as a sheet and confussed. The looks children give when they spill milk. (Uh, Oh.)

"She's gone Sire." So outraged, he turns to Sophie and lifts her off of the ground about a foot. "You fool, how could you let her Escape!" Fingers tightening around her neck as he clamps down and snaps her neck. Tossing her to the ground. Where her body slides into the shadows of the corner. "Eeeek!" Excitement fills the space. He didn't care if it were her fault. Only that her misfortune lay in being in the wrong place at the wrong time. He only cared

Page 116.

that someone pays.

High pitched giggles and snorkles came from the corner she lay in. Good thing she were dead. Or it would truly hurt.

In the shadows lay dozens of his pet munchkins. Chowing down on her flesh and organs under her clothes. Only seconds later the munchkins gave an echoeing burp that shook the room. Then with teamwork they tossed her body back into the light. Clothing, bones and hair intact.

His pets were picky eaters. Their cries are a horrid mixture of hissing, gurgles with ashmatic wheezing sound. Their eyes completely in darkness. Bodies white with a clearless texture. Tongue and body were a mixture of snakes and spiders. The webbing came from the nape of their neck in a design on their headband. Teeth ruggid and full of venomious numbing poisons.

After pacing the edge of his bed for a short while he turned to Gary and Larmain and said. "You two, go search for her." Taking the messenger guard with them. The room fell silent. Delvoir slithered back to the floor then shifted to his human shape. "Master, time was stopped. We followed her and a hooded figure riding to Olivanders Citadel." Another moments pause. "I believe she is still there."

Page 117.

Iolis sat silent for a good long minute thinking of her.

"Oh, I see."

Then sat his face in his palms and waited for more.

"Lycos is watching and waiting."

Something gave Delvoir a look of certainty from within.

"Master, Lycos says that she is boarding The Equidorian Siren and to come quick and claim what is yours."

"Delvoir turn yourself into a huge creature with magnanimus wings, so we might take flight."

While Delvoir was changing shape. Iolis was writing a note for Aiden. Statings all that has happened. Except leaving out where he was going.

General Aiden Mctavish; Urgent, I have left to travel for a while in my forest. I'm sad to say I will not be getting married. I need time to heal from my broken heart. Took my two Padowah. Take care of my dozens or so Munchkins and castle duty's till I return. Sire Of Showknizar, King Iolis. That seemed good enough. Someone was leeking info to betray him. this note would keep suspicion from arrising. Delvoir was ready and Iolis now lookedready to fight and claim what he thought was his.

Page 118.

And Out The Window They Went.

A couple of miles out they decided to stop for sanctuary and time to re-group. Lycos joined them.

"Sire, take this tablet. It will help you claim what is yours without so much as a fight."

Iolis grinned Harshly and Pocketed The Pill.

Now in a pirate disguise. He watched and waited while peeling potatoes. Waiting for her. the door opened to the cabin. Long slender boots, tight pants, rappier and dager belted to her waist by the harness. White fluffy blouse and black vest. Allowing all to see her tanning clevage. Dark Auburn curls wrapped in a lavender ribbon behind her neck. Sun's lighting up her silhouette. She stepped out onto deck and her eyes lit up. Iolis watched Evy secretly all day. Waiting for night to fall and for her to be alone.

Page 119.

The Title Of A Crucified Innocence

Chapter Thirty One;
Dubious Escapade.

Deck of The Equidorian Siren gleamed as the suns warmth kissed the wood. Amazed at what lay outside. Redish canyon scapes. Huge pillars the size of slimmed down volcanoes. Unable to see the bottom. As it was covered in crystal blue water.

Looking further over the banister. Mermaids carrying small spheres of fire on torch sticks. To get a better view of them, Evy rushed to the front of the ship and leaned over the edge.

An under water city surrounding a castle that must have been their capital. Utterly amazing. The life down below looked so peaceful, er... what do they call them here?...

Page 120.

"Sirens."

Evy uttered aloud. Astonished at there beauty. A shoal of them swam by. They all seemed to need to be somewhere. Swimming pretty moderatly. she was entranced. Something Evy didn't expect happened.

The last siren turned and locked his eyes on her. Hunger ripping through it's stomach. It launched itself at Evy Mouth open. Rows of pointy shards headed for her neck. Eyes uncultivated. Black and Empty.

Evy was getting sick of getting the short end of the stick. Something in her snapped. she had, had enough. less than a foot away from her. Evy raised her right hand into a fist. Out of instinct, she defended herself and sucker punched the creature in the side of what resembled a jaw. It's face riccochetting off her knuckles and fell back into the water. Evy backed away from the edge. Bumping into a stunned swash buckling buccaneer. His eyes wide. "I'm truly sorry you had to see that, but I'm kinda sick of being attacked and kidnapped. Living in this world that is cold and full of suffering. I feel like my mind is truly lost and paralized. I hate feeling like a waste. I'm too young. I belong to no one but myself. Where is the Captains quarters?" Stumbling and fumbling over his words. "I saw the siren coming at you in mid air. I came to help you, but I know now you can

Page 121.

handle any situation. His quarters is at the back of the ship. Fancy golden design carved into his door."

With a wry smile he added,

"You can't miss it."

I smiled back.

"Thank you, sir."

Then politely bowing, Evy turned and left. Minutes later Evy found the door and tapped lightly.

"Come in lady Evy Trinity Bridgewater."

The voice was soft and slowly spoken with great patience and wisdom. The cabin room was dark and full of dust that settled on everything. A fragile old gentleman sat in a huge desk chair overlooking tons of maps and papers sprawled out over the desk. Huge window letting warmth flood in. This man looked oddly familiar. The way his jaw clenched and his boney webbed fingers. Evy wished she could remember."Come sit dearest Evy." Evy followed his fingers to one of the two chairs sitting across from him. Picking one, sitting. Leather appolstry squeeking at her movement. The older man giggled. Evy smiled at him a little embarrassed. "My name is Alfizor. Most of my friends call me Alfie." Evy listened patiently.

Page 122.

"You, I hope will become one of my friends. Evy it is my duty to protect you and get you to safety."

"Thank you for your kindness and great generocity. I also hope we can become good friends Captain Alfie."

He smiled whole heartily. Then they parted. Evy went to her room to rest and try to configure all the events in this wacky place.

The Title Of A Crucified Innocence

Chapter Thirty Two;
Uneasy Chills.

Finding Iolis's letter gave off a bad vibe. One that was misleading. Walking over to Iolis's bay window to stare out. A giant flying creature headed toward The Death Forest. Blonde flames flying in the wind. Iolis. Headed to Olivanders Citadel. Turning away from the window Aiden reached for a plate of meat and slid it in the corner. Then he returned to the window. Something inside him twisted and turned his heart. Like a wet rag.

Aiden reached for some silver dust and tosses a hand full out the window. Whistles and dives out. Running down the side of The Dark Castles tower.

Headed for the ground. Running so fast

Page 124.

that as he dives through the dust his body morphing and changing into a Lycon. Dark fur slithers over all his skin. Nose stretches out. Ten feet from the ground he hops off the building, leaping into a loop front flip and landing perfectly on Ithica's back. He lean's forward and whispers.

"Ride yonder Ithica, we need to be to sire Ahckmelutra's pronto."

Ithica moved faster than usual. But since time was against them. Aiden sprinkled some dust on her sides. Black feathered wings grew twenty feet in Comparrison on each side of her. they lifted and were off. Flying through the clouds. He pulled out Iolis's letter to him and re-read it for some clues.

General Aiden Mctavish;

Urgent, I have left to travel for a

while in my forest. I'm sad to say

I will not be getting married. I

need time to heal from my broken heart. Took my two Padowah. Take care of my dozens or so Munchkins and castle duty's till I return. Sire Of Showknizar, King Iolis. Landing Ithica under a similar window to Iolis's. "Wait Lass." Then he stood on her saddle and jumped

Page 125.

onto the wall. Where he landed on his stomach. He pushed himself to his feet and dug up the side of that tower. At the top he jumps through the window head first and rolled into a crab walk crawl.

Up alone in the tower stood Ahckmelutra. Looking at Aiden. Aiden shimmied a cold spurt through the tips of his skin. pulling in his fur and nose. He handed his note to the king and conversed for a while. Debreifing him through the current events of climbing up the building.

"General, we must leave immediatly."

Up to the window flew Sire Ahckmelutra's red scaled dragon. He hopped on. Then up came Ithica after the long necked dragon moved away from the window. Both men seated and flying toward The Death Forest.

They got there too late. But decided to follow the ship. staying near the border of Embala as close as they could, watching and waiting.

Page 126.

Chapter Thirty Three;
Mistaken Identities.

As soon as Eldor rose Iolis waited for Evy to leave her room. He stay's to the shadows. A girl comes out and sit's on deck stairing at the Planet Eldor. Completely conversed in water. But lights up the evening sky. He sneaks carefully behind her while she is in thought. One silent step at a time. "Good, Bate!" As he moves so quick and grasps her neck and snaps it. Killing her instantly. He turns her to face him directly.

"Better to rid me of you before you get to be trouble."

Page 127.

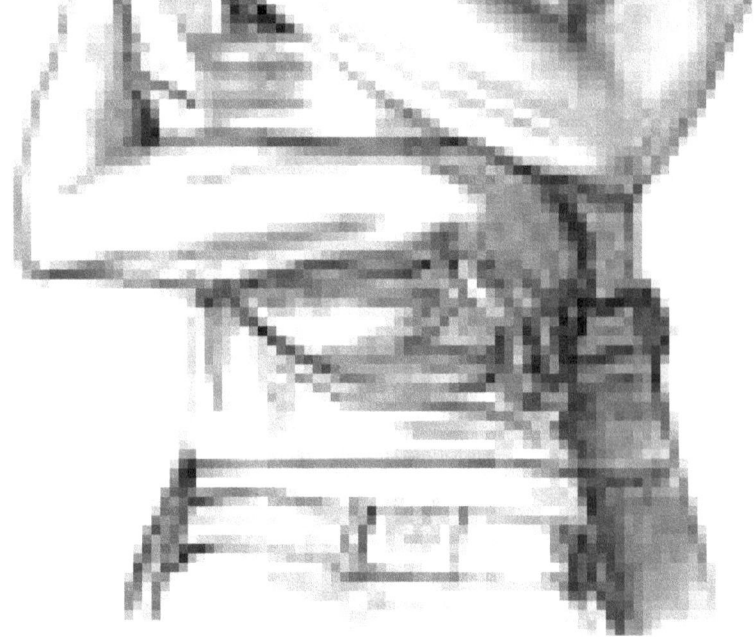

Then tosses her over the banister into the water. He expects a splash. But get's none. Peaking over the edge, he see's the siren who was sucker punched earlier today. Face swollen and eyes orange. Unlike humans. Siren's eyes swell and turn orange when bruised. He caught her and brought her under to Arcmeda. His home to share with family. And Eat.

Iolis sneaks back into the shadows and waits for her again. thirty minutes later light spills from a cabin door onto deck.

Page 128

Chapter Thirty Four;
Beautiful Rememberance.

Evy was passed a note after dinner to meet Gabriella on deck under the waterplanet she called Eldor. Pleased that she made it on deck first. Evy began to think and experiance all the beauty Embala's world had to offer. Stopped at the bannester she looked up at Eldor and all the stars. Flying creatures soar through the night. Peace came over her when she saw a red scaled dragon soar infront of Eldor. Breathing fire and calling for it's mate. Evy couldn't help but think of Aiden. She may dislike his motives and actions. But Evy could never truly hate Aiden.

Page 129.

Looking down over the bannister, Evy could see Arcmeda the underwater castle and city. Glowing torches looked like dancing fireflies in late spring early summer at home.

A smoky substance swirles in the water and a face comes up through it. It's that siren. Eyes changing quickly from orange to black and teeth dripping blood.

It stuck it's hands up onto the ship and started to climb through suction. Evy jumped back when she saw it moving pretty quickly toward her.

Evy wasn't prepared to fight a siren. she was in her night gown. Silky and white low cut. Barefoot, hair undressed gleaming in the light from Eldor.

Page 130.

Chapter Thirty Five;
Deciept.

Watching Evy step out of the light on the deck gave Iolis a rewarding feeling. Shutting the door behind her. Light diminished. She walked over to the bannister. Looking up. Bathing in the light of Eldor.

She looked too lavish. White silk gown hanging to her every curve. Barefoot, hair loose and brushed. All too tempting. Her skin glowing as she stood in thought.

Iolis crept up behind her, tablet in the folds of his middle finger and ring finger. Only a couple of feet behind her. She jumps back into his embrace. Pill going into her mouth as she almost shreiks.

Holding firmly on her mouth and over her

Page 131.

body. Iolis watch the pill dissolve onto her tongue. Neon purple and blue spill from Evy's mouth down her throat.

She struggles as he pulls her into the store room. Fear tingles through her and changes waves and power rippling a lime tint off her skin. the sensation was tantalizing, almost paralizing. It was a rush, Iolis let her go. She turns around and her face lights up but soon changes alarmingly.

"Why did you leave me, How could you leave me with a total stranger."

Iolis knew she was seeing someone else in him. So he played to her rules. "I'm sorry, Evy. I tried to protect you and I couldn't bare to be away from you. Tis no excuse for my actions. I know now I was wrong." She looked up at me. Her brain registering it all. to keep things moving. "Please forgive me. When I'm with you our body's are close. My fingers wandering the great unknown. Kissing you, holding you, touching you Evy. Makes the old me die inside and the new me come alive." She stands on her tiptoes and lightly brushes Iolis's hair away from his eyes. Her own full of love. Iolis never felt love before. She was opening new feelings he never realized were possible to feel. Iolis Imagined the looks he was getting from her, were really ment for him. Her hand sliding up and

Page 132.

through Iolis's hair then down his neck under his ear to caress his stuble on his chin.

She kissed Iolis gentle. He felt cool sparks ripple through his lips. Iolis moved his hands over her curves and down her thy's. Sliding the material up and holding her with her legs locked around his waist. Outside thunder rattled the sky and rain began to pour heavily. Walking her to a stack of unmarked bags, Iolis kissed Evy harder, feeling the passion she was making him experience in her. Sliding inside her, pressing gently at first. Her breathing scattered and learning to deal with pain. Inside her and being part of her, Iolis felt abate. Less of a man. Only pulsating passionate vibes, a god or someone worthy of this woman should feel. Hand moving down her breasts to rest on her abdomen. thrusting as light flickers through the windows showing her even more radiently. Her eyes lighting with flames of florescent purple and blue. Colors showing full of passion. Abetting Iolis to continue harder and faster. She has truely awoken and Iolis was the first to witness as her muscles opened and tightened in a rhythmic beat. Then as he was about to finish. She stretched upward. Grabbing onto Iolis's shoulder and biting down like a primitive animal. Supressing a moan but failing. her fingers and teeth drawing blood. Something happened. Pulling back her

Page 133.

eyes went all black then normal. Her face which held extacy and love for who she thought Iolis was. Twisted into a look of fear and disgusted pain. the tablet was wearing off.

"Tis done Evy, I have taken you. In our world, This was a union of marriage. I told you, I would have you, I stop for nothing as I always get what I want!"

Boy Iolis missed the look Evy held for him before. Full of wanting. But in his eyes, she will learn to Love. As he has made her his. Iolis thought greedily as she turned her green eyes away from his.

Tis done Love.

Page 134.

Chapter Thirty Six;
Time To Rise.

Thunderious lightning shattered webs of white jagged lines across the ruggid billowless clouds that etched across Eldor. Covering as much of it's illuminious water reflection as possible. Leaving no possible light from the stars that hid in fright Loud booming crackled meeting the sight with heavenless noise. On the ship, light emploded waves of lime that rippled to the surface of the ship. Waves pulsating Moving the rushing water in a rhythmic motion. Big reoccuring waves brushing the shore line repedative. The exterior too inferior too notice what was going on. Something was deffinatly wrong.

Taking handfull of magic dust. Shaking it hesitant in his palms.

With thumbs up against his sullen lips. Before anything, Aiden pauses to think. Closing his eyes once more to remember Evy.

Running toward him. Then another with her before him. Cheeks going aflame. He remembers holding her gently against the bookstand and tapestry kissing her gently. then carrying her in his arms down dark tunnels as her head rests against his chest. the lavender and white wine scent fills his lungs as he sucks in the words Alaric Talwayr, then blew. Both his clasped fingers released and pulled apart as far as they could go. To reveal a crow pressing from the balls of his wrists. Pressing further out of Aidens skin. The crow wiggled forward. "Warn her." Was all he has to tell his crow named Alaric in a hushed whisper. For the bird was quickly in flight and on it's way to deliver the humble message. Alaric the crow slithered and skirted past oncoming waves of warm passionate ripples. Dodging with wings spread. Light glistening off of them. Long wrinkled legs pulled in.

"Boom!!"

He crashes into the side of the ship. Vanishing into it's requiem, leaving a dark hazy smoke in it's place.

Page 136.

There Lucinda sleeps, as if she herself were a grand statue of art. Full of beauty and glowing wisdom. Eyes white and eyelids spread open. Images flickered between her crystalline lens's and corneas's.

Seconds before the mushroom boom. She sit's up, eyes still flickering in a dark and unknown place.

"Something is wrong. Fate has misdelt us."

Reaching out and up instinctivly to retrieve the black crow. "Thank you Alaric Talwayr." As the small glistening bird lands on her palm. She slams her other hand down, smashing him back into silver magic dust and black smoke. Then blowing what made him, all over her tiny one windowed room. taking what was left of him and sprinkling the dust above her sillohette. To shrink and grow wings. Then she fluttered through the wall like a ghost. leaving a white dusty cloud in her place. On the otherside she got knocked off balance by the emense tidal wave of wind thrusting her to shore landing in a tree. A bit dazed and confussed. Waves rippled out of the exterior of the ship, then... "Boom!!!" One huge wave shoots and hits all plant life. Similar to a mushroom cloud pushing a huge

Page 137.

gust of wind. Blowing all leaves, dirt and rain everywhere.

The gust slithered through tree's and emense waves on the ocean. All goes dark. One of Iolis's henchman slithers onto the side of the deck. Padowah, shapeshifting from a large snake into a fourheaded flying serpant dragon. Scales glistening in the lightning storm.

Aiden watches as Iolis drags Evy by the wrist like a rag doll. Her skin glowing through her white nightgown. something deep inside of him raising rage to the surface of his skin.

Iolis yanks her ontop of the beasts back. As it's about to raise and leave. It's tail coyly slithers off deck into a sworm of sirens. Ambushed, the beast accidently knocks Evy and Iolis from the sattle. Every siren was preoccupied with the Padowah.

The diversion helped Iolis drag Evy through the murky water unnoticed, crawling toward land.

Page 138.

Chapter Thirty Seven;
        World So Cold.

Evy stared blankly at the very man whom betrayed her. She had given all of herself to this man whom she though she loved. Rage ignited inside her. Filtering through her veins til Evy couldn't conceal or control her most dangerous primal instinct. Disgusted. Her hand swooshed through the darkened storage room to land a perfect smack against his muscular cheekbone. the sound of his skin slapping under her palm made a horrific sound, Evy's never been accustomed to hear.

        Pure stubborness filled him. Evy couldn't see him all too well in the dark. A candle flickered in the edge of the room. His palms clenched around her skin of her shoulders and brought her in for another possessive kiss.

Page 139.

Tears started to trickle down Evy's cheeks as his arms slid further around her tightening.

"Surrender all your dreams too me tonight."

He whispered after kissing Evy.

"No!"

Evy squirmed but couldn't break his embrace.

"I'm losing my patience, You Are Mine whether you like it or not."

Evy finally pushed him off her, knocking her off balance into a pile of stacked sacks of food.

"Open your eye's, you have betrayed my first trust." Looking cynically into her eyes. And, what is that?" Curiosity soon filled over the cynical in his eyes. "You can't have it both ways. You've done some taking, now it's time to give." With that Evy jumped to her feet and tried to rush past him toward the door. Evy's folly decision was thwarted. Fingers almost grasped around the knob. Evy was twirled around, his fingers around her wrist and waist pulling her back to the sacks. Dropping Evy on her knees and hands. "Almost time, I promise." Evy turned her face to Iolis. "Knock me down. I'm bound to get back on my feet again."

Page 140.

His lips raised.

"I know, Thats why I like you soo very much.'

Then without hesitation, he grasps Evy's palm pulling her up to drag her out the doorway into open rain onto the deck. A huge snake morphed into a fourheaded dragon keeping it's slimy tail.

Iolis's grip clenched even tighter around Evy's wrist. Puddles splashed under her feet on the deck as rain showered around them. Iolis pushed Evy onto the great beasts back and crawled behind her on the saddle. The giant monster started to lift off of the deck when they were pulled and shoved off it's back into icy cold murky water. Evy's whole body began to sink. Under the water she watched as the creature was ripped apart under the water. Evy also noticed the thick blades coming from the sirens tail's. Nothing like fairy tales. Shards spiked out of their tails. Slicing through flesh and blood induced water. Some of them opened their mouths releasing three rows of white teeth now stained bergandy. Still sinking lower and lower until Iolis grasps my wrist and drags her above water for oxygen. Evy tried to take her first gulp of air, but get yanked quickly through waves of untame water and blankets of rain sheethed with lightning filtering through the air. Ahead the shore brings partial safety.

Page 141.

Iolis drags Evy to the sand and quickly takes bits from her ripped night gown and ties up her wrists and ankles. Leaving Evy to cry and stay put.

From Evy's view point, she watched helpless as if she even cared if they died. Thats how outraged she felt. Evy hoped they both become sliced pieces of poultry. Another gasp of air and Evy almost caughed up the whole water supply. This is ridiculious. Life from this point on seems pointless. Pain riveted from her body.

"Oh, Lord help me please."

Evy begged, just about to give up on life, splashing waves caught her attention. Glancing down at her feet might have been the worst mistake so far. Webbed fingers clung onto mounds of sand and rocks as it began to crawl toward her. Evy let out a scream that startled even herself.

Page 142.

Chapter Thirty Eight;
Going Down.

More Thunderious sounds shattered the silence of the heaving storms cry's. Iolis quickly bound Evy. Only after gaining a glance of Ahckmelutra. A sinister smile spread over Iolis's face. As he quickly glanced down at his handy knotts on Evy's security. She wasn't smiling. Her eyes only furiated and glinting lime fire. His smile dropped to a frown then pulled back up to a seriously straight line. Now it was time to finish this fued.

"Ahcky, so good to see you. Have you met my new bride?"
Pointing toward Evy with the blade of his sword.
"I will kill you for this Iolis!"
Page 143.

Ahckmelutra spat. Anger flared in his nostrils as fur and steam rose off of his body. Black and yellow flames of fur drenched in rain. Iolis laughed into the oncoming drops of heaven's tears. Iolis's flamed coat and Ahckmelutra's black coat. They both ran daringly at eachother. Swords drawn. Blades sliced through drops of rain. Knocking the tears off course and flying in mid-air. Ahckmelutra would spur Iolis's blade and Iolis would pull all defences then rush him again. Ahckmelutra would also spin in his defences and then also go for the kill only to be defeated. At one point the blades met and held their position. Both not budging. Finally when the pressure was too great, lightning crashed down on the metal and shattered the blades. Knocking them back. The two fueding twins turned to hand to hand kombat. Both bloody and preoccupied with eachother. Angry bursts of lightning touched down igniting different areas of the ground. Tree's split in half and char slid down the trunks leaving drenched seeping paths of disturbed black death behind. All went quiet for the only thing that filtered the air was a blood curtling scream. Both stopped and looked in that direction. Standing between the scream and them was Aiden Mctavish. Hair soaked, eyes piercing blue, beard rough and stubbly catching bits of raindrops. Aiden

Page 144.

flipped his head in Evy's direction. Wanting to help but being stuck between a hard place and a rock.

Chapter Thirty Nine;
Unbearable Desertion.

Blood curtling screams is what rushed past Evy's lips toward the surface. The creature grasped onto her leg and began to pull itself closer to her. It's tail flailing like an excited pupy's. Swooshing through the rain. Terror filled her mind. If only her hands weren't bound and her legs weren't wrapped together. Evy could kick. If they were free.

Arms almost translucent. It's webbed suction cupped fingers tightened like a leach around Evy's ankle. It started to get closer. It's hands started climbing up her legs and onto her outer thys.

The siren was almost completely ontop of her. It wheezed with hunger. Eyes shimmering with delight.

Page 146.

Evy turned her face toward the fight and tried to shimmy away.

The first thing she noticed was Aiden. Eyes wide and longing to help. Evy's heart lifted to the sight of him then sank. Was he the last thing she would enjoy seeing before she died? The wheezing got louder. Evy turned her head back to the siren. Rows of teeth glinted in the lightning. It raised it's head. Mouth wide and dripping with drool. Yellow drool. Some of it's soliva landed right next to her head and began sizzling. It was acid. The ground beneath Evy began to move. The siren was using it's bladed fin to drag her to the water. As it's head began to sink down. Evy cringed. The teeth barred down on her flesh. Warm blood seeped down her skin igniting the ground. Lighting up the creatures face. It's lips resting on her neck. The pain dulled as it's acidic saliva slipped into her blood stream. When it's head raised in delight. His lips drenched and glowing lime. Satisfaction tipped his lips into a horrendis smile. It dipped it's head again. This time sliding it's webbed fingers under Evy and holding her tight. Evy caughed up pain and bits of blood. Everything began to get dizzy. Evy's eyes rolled back inside her scalp. He raised his head once more to scream an unnatural sound. then a blade flickered in the lightning light and took his head clean off. Standing over Evy was

Page 147.

a sight for sore eye's. Lucinda... hair blowing in the rain. Eyes white and tightly wielding a pretty sharp desolate blade.

Page 148.

Chapter Fourty;
  Tainted Love.

When Evy lifted her eyes, she saw Aiden once more lifting her in his arms and carrying her close to his heart. Evy rested her head against him. Water drenched her white silky night gown. And they were close, the moisture between them began to warm up.

Evy locked her arms around his neck as he walked her toward Ithica, or atleast Evy thought it was Ithica. She had gigantic black wings. Drops of rain teetered off of them, making them glisten. On top of her sat Lucinda.

The only thing Evy could say, she remembered were Aiden placing her in the arms of Lucinda and patting the horses behind. Signaling Ithica to leave. Still dazed

Page 149.

and lost. Evy grasped onto Aidens shirt and wouldn't release him. He unclinged Evy, then kissed her and gently rubbed her cheek.

"I will always find my way back to your heart, Evy."

Then they were in midflight. Evy screamed his name as thunder shook the very atmosphere and lightning re-colored the darkened clouds.

"Aiden, Nooooo, Please Dear Lord Noooooo!!!!, Stay with me!!!!"

Evy begged. From a distance, Aiden became as small as an ant. The thing that caught her eyes before stress and loss of blood over took her. Was the sight of Iolis and Ahckmelutra staring blankly. Rain drenching their bruises and cuts.

Looking up at Evy as she left. One last thunderious bolt sent Evy into a overwhelmed slumber.

Page 150.

Chapter Fourty One;
        Emptyness.

Aiden Watched as Evy screamed a most horrific cry toward him. Her hand Extended as she left his view to The Elvin Requiem Sanctuary.

He wasn't really all that concerned about his safety. She was all that mattered. He even kept staring up into the rain and war painted sky. Looking at nothing and everything at the same time.

The thunder closed off all sences as he fell numb to her departure. The last thing he remembered was the cracking noise under the back of his shattered scalp. Cracking under an extent of force.

Page 151.

Chapter Fourty Two;
Revolations

Both Ahckmelutra and Iolis knew Aiden to be a double spy. Although not for eachother. Ahckmelutra sent Aiden to spy on Iolis. But never knew, He himself to also be spied upon by Iolis. But now they knew as it was clearly confirmed. General Aiden Mctavish was a traitor and must be delt with. Iolis spun toward Ahckmelutra. Smile gleaming while devising a perfect plan. "Ahcky, you take him and we'll punish him together. Of course, when we hang him, I want to be seated upon my padowah Lycos to watch the festivities." his lips straightening to a

Page 152.

serious expression as he thought. Then after a minute of listening to his thoughts his face gave a certain misconception that turned his lips upward again. "What malice, do you plan Iolis?" Ahckmelutra felt skeptical of his brothers bouding friendliness. "None, I just don't want to waist such entertainment." Ahckmelutra still skeptical of his brothers devious plans decided to take a chance at trust. Even if it did give him satisfaction. His mind releaved to get some dirty work handled and out of the way. "Okay, Iolis. I see your point. Lets torture and question him together for fun."

Water drenching Iolis and Ahckmelutra's fur as rain poured in emense masses. They whistled for Iolis's remaining Padowah Lycos who soured through the rain to his masters comands.

The Title Of A Crucified Innocence.

Chapter fourty Three;
Oubliette.

The next morning, Aiden woke with a thrashing headache. Not sure of what to make of it. He sat and almost fell back with a shock of dizziness and pain. His head surely bared an emense wound. Eyes blurry to the darkened room. He tried once more to sit and when luck finally prevailed, he scanned his surroundings. He was on a cot, a couple of inches from the ground. Cell bars ancient and iron covered one wall. With a door made up of years of rusty desolation and neglect. Mold and filth filled the musky darkness. A door cracked open on the other side of the barred threshold let a thin strip of light into view. Next to the entrance sat a burroughly old man. Gut hanging out low as his hands cradle it like an expecting mother. Eyes heavy with brown bags of sleep. White beard stretching over his belly like a white waterfall cascading between his legs to sit comfortably on the floor like a blanket. His eyebrows white and sinking over his slumbering eyes like two cotton comforters. Wheezing a snore from his gaping mouth while his nostrils continuously blow bubble's of snot. A gold chain entangled in his white stubbly fingers. The key falling low near his crotch only inches from the dirt floor. Screams bellowed from the hall beyond the opposing door. Rattling the startled old guarding officer awake. Rushing up to his feet, he almost forgot where he was and who he was. "Ting!" The golden chain and dangling key clattered to the floor. After registering everything, He got giddy and grinned. Teeth black and rotting, with white foam seeping from his lips, dripping to the floor. He looked at Aiden then glanced down and reached for the fallen object. Only to place it over his neck. As he placed it upon his neck. The door swung open and in stepped Ahckmelutra followed by Iolis. Ahckmelutra quickly grasped the dangling key off of the old guards neck. Ripping it. The chain so new and sharp, sliced through the man's neck, tearing flesh and bone. Tossing it across

Page 155.

the room, where a huge chunk of his grotesque flesh slapped Aiden across the face. Dribbling down his cheek to fall in a pile of blood at the base of his feet. Aiden quickly brushed the smear of blood off his face with the edge of his hooded cloak's sleeve. Ahckmelutra placed the key in the door and turned it. As it twisted in the lock, more flesh dripped from the glistening chain. "Erk!!" The door opened slowly. In stepped Iolis, folllowed by Ahckmelutra. Both their eyes flashing red and teeth gritted. "So, she has fallen in love with scum as meek and treatorish as you. Aiden." Aiden's head turned down. Eyes glancing over his scuffed boots. His lips turning from a frown then to a smirk as he heard those words of encouragement. "What are you smiling about?, It wasn't ment to happen this way. She was supposed to fall for one of us." Ahckmelutra spat in disgust. Iolis grasped the coller of Aiden's tattered cloak lifting him off his feet and throwing him hard against the wall that broke his fall. "Crack!" Ahckmelutra rushed at Aiden who slid down the wall. Then grasping Aiden's left ankle and wrist lifted him off the ground in a 360 degree spin. Landing him face first into the same shattered wall, cracking his nose. "Who allies with you, Aiden?, Tis Olivander and Alfie isn't it. Where has Lucinda taken Evy?" He screeched like an animal demented. Aiden would not tell them. His lips sealed shut as a locked volt. Finally Ahckmelutra broke and spat out. "Iolis, take this treachorious fool to the Oubliette until tomarrows Execusion by rope!" Out of excited spite, Iolis picked Aiden up and glided the traitor to the hole in the floor. Then pulled him close and whispered. "Tis you she saw, when she surrendered her love and body to me. That aweful ache in the pit of your stomach is your retribution. She will be mine again whilst you rot in your bottomless pit. With the maggots and vermin eating your flesh and nibbling on your broken neck as if it were jerky." Then He drops Aiden into the black abyss. Aidens eyes wide and tears escaped. things seemed to be falling apart for him. He knew how cruel Iolis could be. The thought of him bewitching Evy into seduction was cruel. Anger rose to where his flesh prickled fur and his nose stretched. He could barely control his animal instincts as he thought of any man touching her. His heart also sank to the empty pit of his stomach. For hours he tried to escape the Oubliette. Only to fail at each attempt up the jagged walls. A sliver of light barely touched his eyes, he was so deep it was impossible for a species like him to escape. By the time he excepted fate and the possiblity of ever being released. his animal instincts pulled back as well as his fur slipping back into his body and nose shrinking to human form again.

Page 157.

His piercing blue eyes stung from the fierce tears and many days exhaustion from worrying about Evy, his beard still stubbly and soft moved under his tightening jaw. His shoulder length brownish black hair was tangled and full of sweaty dirt particles. He was tired, sore and on his hands and knees preying for help from anyone. Blood trickled down his shattered nose and cracked scalp dripping down in streams ending in dirt mixed piles beside him. He sat in total darkness. The crate high above his head shared his fate. which was sealed and unable to change.

Finally he rested his head, on his knees and fell to silent slumber. Dreaming of her and the short time they had spent together. He began to repent for all his sins, preying she would forgive him. knowing that her love ment the world to him. His thoughts smiled. Knowing Evy was safe with Lucinda at the Elvin Requiem Sanctuary. Then he was out. All thoughts were blank and everything spun, pulling him away from his reality.

Page 158.

Chapter Fourty Four;

sanctuary.

Rain cold and icy splattered Evy's skin making her eyes flutter open in alarm. Lucinda held Evy tight against her as they continued on their journey. Ithica's wings slowly battered through the rain. Light started to brighten the surrounding sky, but the rain continued on it's course as if the sun's pressence had no effect on the rainy condition. Up ahead Evy see's a wall with rain pelting the side of it, falling slanted. It reminded her of a lake as she would dive head first into it. A standing virtical wall of liquid, this was odd. Rain seemed to slow as it hit it. The wierd thing about it was the thought of maybe rain was falling out of it.

Page 159.

"Behind that wall of water holds The Elvin Requiem Sanctuary, Where time is haulted still. Years in their were merely minutes on Embala." Lucinda's voice was as meek as a humming whisper that trailed off into thought. Lucinda loosened her grip on Evy then slid her hands under Evy's arms. Digging her heated fingers into the flesh of Evy's chest. Inside her cleavage line. Lucinda sqoze, then released and pulled them out of Evy's flesh. Black engulfed her fingertips. Lime glowed as the holes sealed and became solid again. Evy felt pain and utter discomfort as she screamed. A pulsative wave rippled the air coming from her lungs, splitting the wall of water. Where a passageway led into the sanctuary. Inside a forest of sea coral jungle tree's floated in calmness. Huge cyllinderic balls drooped from all branches. Light calm and welcoming drew in Evy's trust. In the center above all the other jungle coral, rested a gigantic ball of captured fire. A webbing cacoon incased it. A single web held tight hanging from empty air. Ithica steadied to a calm as they entered. Lucinda stuck her black fingers in the dark wings of the mare and pulled. Ithica's wings slid off into dust as she then turned and rubbed the dust into Ithica's rear end. Soon a tail curled and Ithica looked like a floating sea horse prancing as if nothing had occured. That amazed Evy.

Page 160.

The Title Of A Crucified Innocence.

Chapter Fourty Five;
Council.

Warm embers filtered the icy chambers of Ahckmelutra as he held council with Iolis. "What location should we end Aiden's speck of life, Iolis?" Voice cold and harsh with jealousy. "Let us do the farewell festivities at your castle, mine is under repair." Iolis's voice danced with jubulance at every syllible. Ahckmelutra stood, then crossed the room to face his courtyard full of slumbering guards under the nights stars. Eldor's water surface seemed to vibrate. The occurance reminded him of tossing a stone across the lake and watching the ripples dance. His back facing Iolis, he nodded "Let us do it here at sunset, then have a masquerade ball to celebrate the beginning of a new era."

Iolis's smile peaked as the firelight lit up his fury locks into yellow flames. His smile sincere as he imagined offing his brother and Aiden. Then to Evy's creamy warm flesh. Her curves bending and forming to his tight muscle's as he imagined her eyes yearning him every which way.

Almighty, he wished she had fallen for him. In truth he seductively concimated their body's into marriage. She was willing until her senses returned, she was furious. He hoped to tame her animal instinct and only let her instincts show during love making.

Iolis glanced down at his new golden Styth, remembering it paused reality. The firelight glistened across it, beaming off his icy eye's. "Tis a splendid plan."

Then Iolis left to his chambers to rest and formulate his devious plan, leaving Ahckmelutra to stare empathetically into the night wind.

Chapter Fourty Six;
Answers?

The wall slithers open like a curtain of blue velvet. Evy reached out to touch the sides as her finger glided across the water, the liquid surface turned to ice drops. They stopped. Alarmed, Evy pulled her hand back to herself. The curtain closed behind them, but liquid water no longer fell. The wall turned to ice drops haulted apart. Frozen tears. Evy felt like she's been here before, but unsure of remembering it. The feeling of home, made her feel comfortable. They were now passing jungle coral that stood one hundred feet tall and fifty feet round trunks, which were half eaten by termites the size of shrimp, with curly lucid fins. One jungle coral was hidden at the base by

Page 163.

yellow and acidic orange water ferns. Ithica made a noise horses make when they try to communicate, although Evy couldn't understand. Her lips pursed as she pushed a taunting gargle and air bubbles drifted from her nostrils. The november ferns lifted and slunk away to reveal a large crack with a wooden plank used for a door. The door opened as a young boy with arms full of jungle coral drift wood tried to exit. The wood touching his nose and covering his lips. He stopped stunned and his eyes drifted over our black horse Ithica and landed on Evy. His eye brow's raised and held on her. He held tight to the wood, but never took his eye's off Evy. her cheeks burned with embarrassment. She looked away out of respect. Evy was always taught never to stare someone down. It was rude and unlady like. Lucinda jumped from the horse and guided them around the shocked young boy. Inside was a large dome room with lights floating around the ceiling. The dome was made of a special kind of glass. Once clear, but the bottom of the dome walls were dipped in dirt. On top you could see the great dome light in the caccoon webbing. Bubbles swam over the dome in unique jubulant movement. In this room sat a throne of gold with sea coral shell's ebbed in designs incrusted around it. Sitting melonchally a small man. Ears pointy and downcast.

Page 164.

Eye's large flecking sparks of neon purple the size of a small begging kitten, with long dark lash's. Smiling a toothless grin, beard ashen and long like soft fluffy rain clouds. His toothless grin smiling as he greated us. "Ah, Mistress, we have been waiting for your return for a long time. Unfortunatly time has slipped through our fingers. You seek answers and I am here to take you to your hearts desires. Come Mistress, don't be afraid. Lucinda will be waiting for your return. Follow me." Uncertainty clouded Evy's thinking. she turned to Luci, and waited for her approval of Evy's safety. "Evy, we don't have much time, so move fast and open your mind to infinite possibilities. You must never doubt yourself, Now go." Evy turned to leave and Luci grabbed her left hand and whispered. "Hurry for all our sakes." Then released her. Evy hurried to follow the small elvish man down a hall to a large door then stopped. The door startled her, it all seemed eeriely familiar. It was eligant under all that thick layer of dirt. The elvish man looked up at Evy and said. "All your questions will be answered, the truth lies behind the blue veil curtain." Then he left Evy standing their in thought. Evy touched the door with her fingertips and pressed slightly. The door slid into the frame then split in two and pulled apart. Astonished, Evy stepped into the room in awe. It was dark, dusty and possibly dangerious. Curiosity killed the cat, so Evy stepped cautiously.

Hanging from the ceiling a chandelier, it's ancient crystal's burried in coral vermin and water crustations. A bed, dusty and disheveled sat to her right. Next to it sat a makeup table and armoire thickly covered in debri's. To Evy's left on the wall sat a blue velvet curtain. Looking around the room, suddenly gave it a dome shape. Evy took the material and slid it off the wall. Under it sat a mirror. It looked as if one point the walls were covered in mirrors. Slowly Evy's image startled her, The face shifted grotesquely. her eye's darkened to a uniquely eerie demonic shape. her mouth, white did the same. Startled Evy stepped away from the mirror. Webs clung to everything, even her as she stopped moving. Evy averted her eye's away from the mirror to brush away the webs. "This used to be my dressing room. I think you remember the time we spent together in it." The voice was cool and detached. "Times were different, more primal." The voice went on talking. "You know who I am. They prophesized our return. Your return Evy." The reflection relished in that statement. "Who are you, can you help me understand what I must do next?" The reflection smiled then said. "My name was Lorily. You are the reincarnation of me Evy. Fate has your life already planned out. Most seem to think history will repeat itself. But infact You were born to change the rules and tempt even the god's. You have the ability to defy all logic."

Page 166.

"I don't understand, what is it I must do?" The reflection laughed and the room started to turn cold. "You, must follow your heart. I have followed you since you picked up the lex and it's alarming activation sent you from the island of Nori to Ahckmelutra's front lawn. You obsorbed it through contact. It sent you from my home Eldor to Embala." "What are you talking about, that obsered paper blowing in the wind?" Her Eyes made contact with Evy. "Yes, but I suspect you knew I was watching you, when you caught me spying upon you when you first woke in Ahckmelutra's castle. I sent Aiden to change your future. To ensure you had a future and a choice, I was never able to make." "That was you?" An anguished sigh escaped Evy's lips as she thought back to being startled by Lorily's ghost. "You are the Lex and must follow your heart, now turn to my armoire and pull out a dress for your masquerade ball." Evy turned and walked over to the armoire and opened the doors. Inside stood a sparkling white dress with a hint of turquoze. Evy turned back to the mirror to ask one more question. "Why?" was what left her lips. "Because it was written. You need to saduce both Iolis and Ahckmelutra to obtain two parts of a key then follow your heart to finish your conquest. Also you need to

Page 167.

somehow obtain Aiden's Styth. "If you believe, your abilities will assist you in certain situations." The room started to shift making Evy dizzy. Dirt dissapeared from the mirror's, bed and furniture. The chandalier shed the filth and was glowing warm. Evy's mind was frazzled as her body lifted into the air. She began to spin, the mirrors turned so fast it was a haze. Soon it all stopped and Evy was set down on the ground, but her outfit changed and her hair was fashioned for a masquarade. Evy's mask delicatly resting over her nose. Sparkles dusted her cheeks. The slippers She was wearing were dainty and fashioned from an expensive material. Evy had sea shell clips that sparkled through out her auburn tresses. Evy glanced back at the mirror then Lorily said. "Now's our second chance to make everything right, now go and follow your heart, I will forever be with you guiding you toward safety." Evy bowed and thanked Lorily then out the door frame she went, when Evy turned, the room was the same as when she first entered Mirror hidden behind the blue velvet cloth. Evy stepped over the threshold and the spliced door closed and fixed itself as if nothing had occured. "How Odd?" Evy said aloud then returned to Luci who greated her with a warm hug. As she touched Evy, her body stiffened. Whispering "Aiden is to be sent to the gallow's by sunset as the masquarade begin's." Evy held her softly. Page 168.

"I know what I must do if you'll permit it?" She pulled back slightly to gaze into Evy's eye's. She could easily see her reflection in Luci's piercing white eye's. "Of course, what is it?" Evy smiled wryly. "I'm going to follow my heart."

Page 169.

Chapter Fourty Seven;
Dawning Of A New Era.

Warm Embers of Embala's sunlight glistened around Ahckmelutra's grass, signalling for the party to begin. Ahckmelutra sat in his best dressed and waited for Iolis to give signal from Lycos's back. Boredom creaced his eye's as he waited impatiently. The sun's set, torches were lit, guests were dressed and having a ball. Aiden's neck was being fitted. Ahckmelutra stood at Iolis's signal and began his speech. "This traitor is under treason for being a triple spy and harboring the propherical girl. Tis the end of one era and the dawning of a new..." As he said those words he was about to drop

Page 170.

the signal for Aidens strangle. But he saw something that could well persuade him otherwise. Ahckmelutra had no doubt that his brother had seen her also. He turned to Iolis but he was gone. Looking back at Evy, White dress sparkling with a turquoze tint. Everything about her made his heart skip beats.

Chapter Fourty Eight;
Sacrificing The Gallow's.

Coming through the clearing Evy saw Iolis on his dragon and Ahckmelutra, hand in mid-air. Evy's eyes followed his hand to Aiden. Seeing him beaten up and in danger made her heart skip beats, Evy rushed up to the podium. Ahckmelutra stood in shock. Evy dropped to her knee's and begged him not to end Aiden's life. "Please Sire, I beg you not to end his life. Please, swap our places, let him go free. he has family, I will sacrifice myself, I'll do anything. Please." Not a second waisted, Ahckmelutra glanced at Aiden and said "Release Him." As soon as the rope slipped off Aiden's neck he rushed to Embrace Evy. Whispering frantically.

Page 172.

"How could you?" Evy held him tight. "blame it on me, maybe they needed to be wanted. What if I die without you, I couldn't go on. I followed my heart and I wouldn't change a thing. I Love You Aiden Mctavish." Fighting her emotions, Evy almost lost all composure as her temperature raised in disguist over her next dutiful objectives. maybe Evy needed to be wanted, but only by Aiden. "I was used and wronged. Betrayed, promise me you will ride Ithica far away from here to safety." I promise is all he had to say. But he didn't, he pulled out of their embrace and kissed Evy passionatly. Sparks of fate ignited from her lips to his.

He sprang to his feet and darted toward The Truscan Forest toward Ithica, his promising black beauty.

The Title Of A Crucified Innocence.

Chapter Fourty Nine;
Two Worlds Apart.

Ahckmelutra watched Aiden rush from Evy's side into The Truscan Forest. The only thing that came to his mind was (Coward). After Aiden was gone from view. He walked toward Evy, bent low and pulled her into a hug. Whispering gently. "You are brave, and I'm truly sorry. For Everything." He helped her stand, but still kept her enclosed in his warm embrace. People seemed to be watching until Ahckmelutra looked up and caught glances. Music started playing, soft and melodic. Evy still in his arms, he decided to take her and start dancing. Holding her, gave him butterflies. He twirled her and even caught a smile and a giggle from her. Soon after,

Page 174.

he gently led her to his chambers.

Firelight throwing waves of warmth and light gently across the room. The mood was set as he turned her back toward his bed. Gently brushing auburn tresses away from her face. Unclipping each coral clip, then kissing the spots where the clips used to hold tight. Ahckmelutra takes her chin and raises it to gently remove the mask and kiss her. Sparks of passion flutter through his lips.

He pulls up for air then picks Evy up and sets her softly on the matress. Loosening her bodice, undressing her with his eyes. Then continues to kiss her while climbing partially on top of her. Sliding his fingers over her plump curves then behind her back lifting her closer to his heated chest and bulging cock. With his other hand, he slides up her skirts. Lifting her thy's, pulling her closer. Ready to take what was rightfully his. He meets her fingers between her legs as she reaches up and caresses the bulge through his pants. She notices the arousal in his rolled back eyes. Then the flames of passion over come him, and she knows she must be ready for his pounce. Reaching his head down. Lips and tongue circling the tip of her nipple. She almost feels nausiated, but she does what she needs to do. Kissing up her neck toward her flushed cheeks and her honey flavored mouth.

Page 175.

He dives for a kiss then thrusts. She pulls her fingers to his temples. Whispers "I'm Sorry." His eyes fill with confussion. She blows, lime pulsating waves curse into his temples. Knocking him out cold. She's stuck under him, pinned down by his erected cock. His weight all around is blocking her escape. She lay's there for a moment gawking up at Sire Ahckmelutra. Eye's black and vacent. Mouth gleefully smiling. How wry.

Page 176.

Chapter Fifty;
Love For Only You.

Something creaks open and a pressence steps into the room.
"Another minute and I might've had to kill him, for touching you Evy."
Aiden's brogue accent made Evy's blood tingle in anticipation. "Aiden please, help me. I'm pinned and very uncomfortable."

Aiden hoisted Sire Ahckmelutra off of her, tossing him aside as he slid off his silky sheets and onto his bed. "Since he's the youngest brother, he has the smallest bit to the key." Aiden couldn't help but notice her shirt lay open and skirt cranked up to her upper part of her thy.

"Excuse me while I get modest." Aiden

Page 177.

looked down at the crazed fool on the floor. Surprised that prince ass didn't land on his penis and brake it in half or even off.

Aiden reached the necklace on Ahdmelntra, yanking off the medalion and handing it to Evy. "Love we need to leave, I have a place for us to go until the heat is off." Evy's eye's lifted to his and she stepped near him and reached for his neck to pull him down for an intimate kiss. "I asked you to promise me you would leave to safety and you needn't hear my warning, I ask you not because I want to boss you into doing what I say, but meerily because I love you and hold you very dear to my heart. I missed you, and now find my heart skips as I'm still missing you even though you are here and in my embrace. Thankyou, I Love You."

They sneak out of the chamber through the passage way Aiden had entered through the shelfs.

Page 178.

The Title Of A Crucified Innocence.

Chapter Fifty One;
         Devious Ratt's.

      Plan's were beginning to fall in place for Iolis. As he watched Evy being escorted to Ahckmelutra's chambers. He was sure she had a plan for Ahckmelutra. A devious one at that, so he hid behind the mirror and watched, teeth gritted as he bared Ahckmelutra with his bride.

      It was almost unbearable, he even caught himself from jumping out from behind the mirror and decapitating his younger twin. He nearly crept out like a wild man in a jealous rage as his brother almost thrust his man hood into his Evy. Green lime glowed at Ahckmelutra's temples knocking him out ontop of Evy. Whew, was all Iolis could release, he continued to take

Page 179.

in the event. Evy layed trapped, It was almost comical. The gentleman part of him wanted to assist his fallen beauty. But at the corner of the room Aiden skirted around a bookstand ebbed in the wall, Iolis listened to Aiden rumble about Ahckmelutra, and he couldn't have agreed more. Iolis wished Ahckmelutra landed on his penis and broke it off. He laughed in his mind's eye.

He also listened to Evy and Aiden's conversation over her asking him to promise of safety and how he defy'd all odd's to come back for true love and rescue her from that scary erection. He did wish he were for the first time in Aiden's shoes for Evy's sake. But that also made him despise the bastered even more with blinding jealious rage.

But for Evy's sake he would hold his position and temper until later. Soon Evy and Aiden left. Iolis stepped out from around the mirror and closed it behind him while gazing at his barbaric handsomness. Then He pulled Aiden's golden Styth out of his pocket and turned it backwards and activated a transmitter. He Followed through the mirror cautiously tailing Aiden and his beloved Evy.

The Title Of A Crucified Innocence.

Chapter Fifty Two;
         Passionate Rain.

Rain padded against the Carriage sides. Making a peaceful lulling that brought Evy's eyes to a close. She was leaned into Aiden's warm Embrace. He held her and whispered poetry from his land as she fell into a slumber of their intwining passion. She slunk into his embrace even tighter. "No matter where life takes me, Aiden I will always Love you, even if danger follow's, I will fight for our love." He listens to her with great patience and understanding. "aye Lass, My dearest Evy, where I go you will be there with me, forever now. We will be together, until the end and even after." She pulled up to kiss him wickedly. "Thankyou, I needed to hear that from your lips."

Soon the carriage stopped in front of a little pub in Shreve Grove called The Towering Twin's Inn. "Aiden, I would travel a million miles to come to your rescue, you know that right." "aye lass, and I you."

Page 182.

Chapter Fifty Three;
          HomeWard

Lulling toward shreve grove. Pines and cedars shivering tears that fell from Eldor's surface. Soft mist started to cover the spliting path. the path that turned right, headed toward the red cracked barn. the path that led left, around thick brush, toward a two story european town house. drenched in ivy vines and leafs. Columns held up a balcony above the front doors. Two french doors opened onto the landing. Two sterling silver knights stood in the yard. Holding lances pointed at eachother. Two silver rings connected from both lances to hold up a tomb stone slab from top and bottom with black ink etched in vivaldi cursive. Written in english it read...

The Towering Twins Inn.
Smoke silently crept from the slumbering inn, slowly raising toward thick soft curtains of clouds.

Page 183.

Chapter Fifty Four;
Devistations.

Slowly the door creaked under Evy's fingertips. As she closed it, the hallway light diminishes into empty un-used air. She turned around slightly, finding Aiden standing in the center of the bed chamber.

Aiden's sillohette standing calm and peaceful, His head turned slightly catching her staring at him. Their eyes met and a spark ignited her very onset.

The Passion Evy felt, could not alone explain that there is more to life than what they have known. Out of a possessive eagerness, She walked moderatly toward him and took what was hers. Grasping him around the neck and igniting the love Evy felt and ampliphying it tenfold.

Their shared kiss was pure fire and their lips so

Page 184.

tight together, almost signifying no end. As if they were one single passionate being. His hands slid down Evy's sides to lift her skirts to hoist her legs up and around his waist. Evy's legs locked. His palms gently cupping the bottom of her buttocks. For but a single moment they both broke and came up for air, releasing their lips. He lost balance and her back fell into the wall, pain shot through her limbs, but the passion Evy felt was much stronger. A giggle slipped passed her lips.

Time Slips Into Pause

Stepping through the mirror as the shadows easily coerse Iolis's escapade. From behind his back he pulls out his Abso twin golden daggers. both locked together into one dagger. The blade sliced through Aidens rib cage to appear equally deadly, clinging to the dripping flesh. Slivers of candle flame reflected, dancing off of the gold blood induced daggers. Suddenly the tips started to melt down into small worms, slithering under his flesh up his neck toward his brain. As his brain clicked off, his eyes slid shut dulling towared empty decadence. The worms started sliding down his neck back toward his chest. Sliding back into place between his grotesquelly eerie ribcage. Soon the dagger sliced through more flesh, eating cuts till Iolis pulls the twin daggers out and

Page 185

Aiden's body crumbled toward the floor.

As his body fell, his spirit remained piked on that dagger. Iolis holding the handle, he pulls it toward the mirror and moved Aiden into it, Holding him captive for all eternity.

Sliding the styth dyle back into place closing off all exits toward the mirror world and starting time.

Time Slithers To Play For A moment Evy got dizzy sitting there on the longated dressor, legs spread, back arched. heat cursed up her body leaving a cold sweat, that made her more modest parts show their hardest vulnirable side. Evy waited for Aiden to step back into her yearning embrace. The candle that once lit the room had distinguished, leaving it crisp and cold. Evy's breathe seemed to transform into heated smoke. For a moment she started to worry. "Aiden?" Evy whispered out. Suddenly He stepped forward, rushing to her embrace. Kissing Evy as if they weren't just a moment ago kissing. His palms worked down under her butt, to lift her up again as he moved them toward the bed. Before Evy lie back, he takes both his hands behind her back and ripps the material open. Evy slides out of it. His hands bundling the masquarade dress into a colorful bundle, tossing it onto the floor. As it landed something under it gurgled.

Page 186.

"What was that?" Evy's heart pounding fear.

"Nothing my dearest Evy!" fear crawled up her skin. Evy's body tightened.

"Who Are You?" She asked

"Why I'm your husband."

Evy tried to inch away but his palms grasped her ankles and drug her further under his heated body. "You smell exactly what I remember, Love." Taking a huge whiff of Evy into his barbaric lungs. She wiggle to try and get him off but, it didn't work. "I will scream, if you do not let me go!", "The Hell you will! "He grabs a piece of cloth from his back pocket. Something falls out of it, but he doesn't care. "Where's Aiden..." Gets muffled. He takes the fallen object and places it right back into his pocket. "You aren't going to escape again. This time I take you the way, you see me. Because I cannot bare another moment without being a part of you." Evy looked up in his eyes, knowing what he wanted. She also was feeling deeply ill thoughts about what might've happened to Aiden. Evy tried to wiggle away again, then she felt his body tense, as he grasped both her wrists and held her down against her will. Leaving Evy to stare up into his devious eyes. "Okay Iolis"

Page 187.

Evy whispered past the cloth in her mouth, Evy knew he heard her because his head sunk down and he soon took control. His kiss was pure ice, full of possessive passion. He moved around so that our body's would mesh. He was different this time, more gentle, less persistant. Iolis took his time, and Evy let him. One thing kept running through her mind, the key. If she could get it, Evy could escape and find Aiden and they could search for Ashton. Iolis's touch started an icefire that sent shivers up Evy's spine, that started to confuse her heart and her mind. Naked Evy lie pinned under Iolis, heat started to sizzle off of him. She swooned and let him take control. soon his control of passion broke as he slid between her legs. sliding in and out, gradually going from gentle to rough and more persistant. his sweat sizzled and every once in a while Evy would glimpse a patch of fur lifting on his arm or back. Then it would suck in and be gone, Evy's mind was truly playing tricks on her. Climaxing was different for Evy this time, seeing as she was not drugged, or dupped. Although Evy did feel like a dirty old cloth being used over and over again. His release sent millions of magical sensations rippling to the surface in the form of cool drops of ice. Ice that popped and sizzled at the surface. The look in his icy eye's showed that he felt the same sensations and was pleased at what he had conquared. He smiled, and

Page 188.

Evy couldn't help but think of Aiden and the dishonor she felt she had opened up. Evy didn't deserve Aiden, but she sure yearned him like a second half of her soul. Evy would surrender everything for him. "Well Love, I think we have over stayed our due." He jumped up to his feet and pulled on his trousers, and coat. Then he turned toward the disheveled longated dressor and lit a couple of candles. The room was a disaster, and something moved in a jerk on the floor. Frightened Evy grabbed a sheet and wrapped herself and was on her hands and knee's gawking over the disheveled comforter. Eye's focused on the floor. Curiosity was something that, Evy wish she was born without. Evy leaned low and causiously pinched the turquoze masquarade gown with her fingers and lifted. her heart sank. Evy jumped from the bed toward Aiden, blood gooshing from every crevise, the floor was sticky and reaked of blood. her whole body landed next to him and Evy held to him crying, her lungs burned as a realization of not being there for him and having to live with him dieing in her arms. Nothing mattered except for him. Evy screamed and Lightning from the frolicking storm screatched out her whales of dispare. Tears dripped down her face and drenched his dieing shell of a body, Evy looked up at Iolis, who was stunned and in shock."

Page 189.

Help, please. I cannot let him die. Please, Iolis, I don't want to lose him. I will do what ever you want, please don't let him die, I love him, I fear I'm losing him and he is slipping away." Evy turned her face back to Aiden, tears blinding her sight."Aiden, Please stay with me, I know we can win this. I don't want to lose you now, not ever again."Pain rivveted through her heart as his eye's stayed dull and empty, Evy held tight preying to anybody to listen to her prayers. "Evy, He's been dead for quit a while."Evy looked up at Iolis, in disbelief at his inhuman disgression. His finger pointed toward a mirror standing a couple of feet away. The mirror was blank but soon changed, something was hitting against the glass pounding both fists, screaming. All this was too much for Evy to handle. Evy sank down and began cradling Aiden's body again in her arms. Iolis was furiated that Evy was soo attatched to a treatthorious mongrel. He glided toward Evy and pulled her up onto her feet, she resisted then passed out, from full shock. Lucky Iolis caught her before she fell and caught a concussion. He wrapped her up then walked her toward the mirror and pounding spirit of Aiden."General Aiden Mctavish, She is mine and You are inadiquit to sustain a being of form, You will never have her now, lets watch as the maggots and vermin eat at your flesh and turn your neck into a form of delicious jerky, farewell foe."

Page 190.

Iolis jerked the styth dyle backward and stopped all of time, then He carried Evy through the mirror world toward his Home. The Dark Castle.

Page 191.

Chapter Fifty Five;

Screams.

The sun's of Embala rose to light every darkened corner to fill them with warmth. Little William Shaw tiptoed through The Towering Twin's Inn. His mother Mary Elizabeth Shaw and father Gregory Thomas Shaw had instructed him that checking the unoccupied room's would ensure well housekeeping standing and a raise in allowence. The hall's were dark and cold, still shivering off the night's untame events. Every room was cold and a tad bit dusty and unused. The last room at the end of the hall beckoned his attention. The door was icy as his fingertips edged it open,

Page 192.

light filtered through the curtains. His eye's met a huge disaster and disheveled sheet's. Walking toward the bed, William's foot bumped into a covered object, catching his curiosity. He bent low and pinched the burgandy stained white sheet, lifting it. To recieve a huge whiff of Death that slid through his lung's. Light bounced from the window off the mirror to illuminate the travisty releasing such a sorrowful stench. Dried blood left a chaotic puddle across the wood panneling and partially climbed the carpet. The body was almost unrecognizable, shocked he dropped the material and rushed out of the room, down the hall. Throwing himself down the stairs knocking himself off balance into his mother and father. Gregory was unsure of why his son fled the room. William full of terror barely got out a word, as his father and mother rushed up the stairs toward the last room on the left. Gregory used his walking stick to pick up the material. Lifting it up to reveal a half eaten Aiden Mctavish Mary Elizabeth Screamed with horror then swooned to almost fall flat on her face. Gregory rushed to grab her from falling. Holding her as she cried in unstoppable moans and unbareble heaves of distress. Her eye's cascading a wall of water that left her defences to drench down her cheeks into his cotton material. She Cried Why over and over until she

Page 193.

could no longer speak, and closed herself off from the world.

Page 194.

Chapter Fifty Six;
        Honeymoon Of Hell.

Evy's eye's swelled with tears, when she opened them up. A slight overcast of smuldering pink clouds lay dormant against the sun's of Embala. A black silky nightgown covered her curve's. A huge black comforter rest ontop of her chilled form. Cocoa covered wood lifted off of the bed into a square shape above Evy's head. Holding curtains of midnight blue and a green coiled snake. Evy lifted the covers from her feet and sat up. A golden thick chain tied to her left ankle, left her stunned. Why was she being treated like a prisoner? The coiled snake slipped from the post to transform into a man, barely covered by a masqualine loins cloth

Page 195.

that held fast to it's post.

Evy's mind was blown, with eye's wide and a mouth that hung low, stunned was an understatement.

He climbed up onto the bed, eye's blazing, pushing evy back onto the bed and started to selfeshly mis-handle her.

"Sire Iolis, Is gone for a while, and I see no harm in tasting your whole being."

Panicking, Evy turned to crawl up toward the darkening pillows, grasping for something. Anything.

He Pulled Evy to face him, just as she turned, her hand pulls forth a hidden metalic dagger. Slicing through his flesh. Knocking his head clean off into a caged darkened corner, where squeel's and a shiny golden trinket glitter in the dim hours of the evening.

The sounds frightened Evy, yet the glitter caught her attention. Frightened Evy might be, intrigued she was most certainly.

The head that slid in the corner, was thrust back out with an unexcited burp, and growl for more. When the head rolled out, it had no flesh, or eye's. Just hair. Which kinda freaked Evy out yet gave her an amazing idea.

Page 196.

Chapter Fifty Seven;
                Contemptions.

Hazy firelight crept across the darkened carpet of the Foyer. Iolis only felt chills as he thought about the emotions creaping from one teple to the next slipping through his veins to his black heart.

It was wierd, how he suddenly felt so much remorse over Evy's lover Aiden dieing. He wished that for a split second he could bring Aiden back, to see her beautiful smile raidiating again. something unsettling just wouldn't let him relaxe in his glorious victory over her. The light started to slumber into untantilizing crisps of sparks, slowly dieing to empty ash. He closed his eye's in thought.

Page 197.

Chapter Fifty Eight;
    Souless Attempts.

What Evy was about to perform was just as tempting as death at
this point. Revultion for this creature, but more from having to drag his dead
carcus around to do her biddings. Evy didn't know how she did it, she prey
thanks it was a miracle. Knocking his lifeless body to the floor, blood
gooshed everywhere. Mighty fearful of what the noise might bring. Evy
crawled off the bed and measured the chain from the bed post toward her
ankle. It gave her atleast ten feet of space. Some evening light shadowed the
deep corner of the room. Evy pushed his body inch by inch, till they
reached the dark depth of the caged corner. What ever lay in the

Page 198.

cage gave off twittering movement. Finally Evy rolled the snakeman into the corner, and sworms of translucent spider snakes covered his darkened skin, eating fast, giving Evy enough time to snatch what ever lay's in that barred prison. Evy grasped her fingers around the glittered object, and pulled. A small yellow coiled rope was tied to the end. Evy pulled fast, when finally it let loose, she turned to pull herself out of the cage and caught millions of empty spaces where eye's would be, staring hungry at her. Out of nowhere they lept from the remains for her. Evy pressed her left hand in the air in a defensive task, and a hazy smoke burst from her palm and torched the hungry little monsters into sulferic ash. A quick look around, left her breathless. Evy crawled toward the bed, crossing paths with the dead carcus. His body free of skin, muscles and internal organs. left with only his cloth and hair, luckily his head lay right next to his body. A mean gust of wind burst through the curtains and swept the ash and the floor of his remains turning them into grey sand particals, lifting them from the room and back out the window. The blood that was flung everywhere, seeped through the floor boards, not a trace was left and that in itself was odd. Well Evy's luck was picking up, or so she thought. Evy has two parts of the key, now all she needed was the Styth that belonged to her late beloved Aiden.

Page 199.

The sun's set, closing off all light to the bedchamber. A few seconds pass in complete darkness. A gush of wind swish's past Evy. Within a moments hesitation, the fireplace come's to life, lighting the room up and bringing her warmth.

A large pounding sound moves down the hallway headed toward the door to the chamber Evy was in. The door swings open and in steps a man whom make's Evy cry. Iolis; face warn with exhaustive lines and full of wearyness.

Page 200.

Chapter Fifty Nine;
        Fool's Who Never Learn.

He steps closer to the bed. "Ah, My Love. I see you are awake." Revolted by his words. "I Am Not Your Love." Fire erupted from his once Icy eye's. "You are whether you want to be or not." He lept onto the bed and headed for Evy. Iolis watched as she figited and wiggled away from his yearning fingers. Crawling hastely up to the pillow's, finding his Twin Blades. Evy turned as he was ontop of her. Blades glistening under his pinned neck, blood trickling down through gold. Iolis pull's back quick and grasps both Evy's hands, holding the burgandy stained gold while licking cowlisly. Tongue mocking her. Unable to stand looking at his feverish features. Still holding Evy's arms above her head. "Evy, I yearn for you!." He whispered seductivly into her

Page 201.

The Title Of A Crucified Innocence

Chapter Fifty Nine,
Fool's Who Never Learn.

He steps closer to the bed. "Ah, My Love. I see you are awake." Revolted by his words. "I Am Not Your Love." Fire erupted from his once Icy eye's. "You are whether you want to be or not." He lept onto the bed and headed for Evy. Iolis watched as she figited and wiggled away from his yearning fingers. Crawling hastely up to the pillow's, finding his Twin Blades. Evy turned as he was ontop of her. Blades glistening under his pinned neck, blood trickling down through gold. Iolis pull's back quick and grasps both Evy's hands, holding the burgandy stained gold while licking cowlisly. Tongue mocking her. Unable to stand looking at his feverish features. Still holding Evy's arms above her head. "Evy, I yearn for you!." He whispered seductivly into her

Page 201.

repetative way. He moved his lips to consume all of her. Evy almost felt lost for a moment. "Get off of me." she mumbled then struggled some more. His lips raise, with eye's overcast in smuldering passion. Iolis's lips creased to a smile. "You are my bride, and if you will not grow to appreciate all that I have done for you, For us. Then I shall show you." This time he crushed his lips into hers, pressing Evy further into the mattress. His body rigidly tight against hers. Heat burned off his skin, making it unbearable to stand. He flung the daggers, abling to free his hands to grasp onto her. His hands digging unhumanly deep into her flesh, making bruises and filling Evy's palms with blood that trickled from the wounds on her wrists. He pulled up and licked the blood from her, smiling more greedily. dripping off his lips and down his chin. Sharp white teeth glinted down at her. Fur spread over his body leaving his hands stretching to claws. A thick layer of black slid across his eye's. His nose twitching outward to produce a snout. Teeth larger than Evy noticed before. Iolis, or atleast she still thought it was him, took in some deep breaths than arched his back and lifted his emense head up to Howl then snarled a growl. Her eye's wide, frightened, Evy's nerves were seriously shot. It must somehow be possible, or her eye's and brain were playing tricks on her.   Page 203.

Evy screamed and struggled to move away. But Iolis held her down and when he was done frightening Evy, he shook off the beige fur and a mist spread over him as he moved back to his human form. Laughing in deep tenor, he pulled her up to sit next to him. Iolis's smile slowly fading as reality faded into his thoughts. "I don't know what's wrong, I used to be soo sure of what I wanted and how my feelings worked. Since last night, things have changed. I feel remorse for things I haven't even done yet. When I looked in the mirror, My whole body changed, like a piece of me that was missing but never known to be gone, filled the empty pit. Now when I see other's, I feel as though I care what they think, and about their well being." His hands covered his exhaustive face. "I've not lied to you, I have never known the touch of love you showed me when I decieved you the other night. I wish that I could feel it once more to fill that empty pit with something worth living for." Evy felt pity for the man. She took his hands in hers and gently caressed them, listening to his plea's for help. His eye's turning dreamily. Almost in disbelief. Evy lifted his knuckles to her lips, caressing them gently with her small kisses. Slowly they slid away and rested on her love handle's. Evy moved up next to him, that he felt her breath, tickling his timid finely muscled neck.

Page 204.

Claw marks on Evy's wrists sealed shut, leaving but a small smear of blood on her skin. Taking his face in her palms, Evy pulled him close, "It will be alright". Kissing him deeply. His worry some moans drift like ocean currents.

Evy slipped her thy over his seated lap. So lost he was in denial, Evy could not let him go. Parts of him were taking over her. His lips crisp, cool and soft against her's.

Now seated upon his lap, his left hand slid down Evy's lower back, caressing in circular motions. Lavender, blue and lime sparks erupted from the inside of her cornea's. His right hand gently rubbing Evy's ear, cheek and hair line.

Slowly Iolis lifted Evy up to set her beneath him. Iolis's body now resting between her spread thy's.

The night consumed all of their folly decisions, calmness erupted from long desired passion.

Page 205.

Chapter Sixty;

Reverence.

Lingering sparks flicker jubulently off of the icy fireplace, like dancing delicate bubbles leaving a soft glow tingle through the darkened room. Slowly seeping closer to the edge of the bed. Evy lay in thought, confusion bearing down on her heart. wanting to escape, but being torn between her growing feelings for Iolis and her constant betrayal to Aiden. Outside weeping fluffy white clouds turned florescent in the light from Eldor; stars glittered even brighter. Some turned to streak the sky, Evy thought about wishing, but knew such childish things were impossible.

Page 206.

A huge deffining flash ignited her curiosity. Passing through the sky, entering the room through the window, crashing into the flickering sparks. A silent explosion glinted into a misty rain smelling smoke that swirled down the bed post toward the chain tightly secured around her ankle. Evy couldn't hear the click but felt the reverberence of it unfastening. The smoke felt like a delicate chilled hand, more feminane then masquiline.

"Get Up!"

Silence then...

"Get Up!"

The meek humn of a stern whisper filled the silence with unrealism.

"Huh?" Evy murmered toward the darkness. "Get Up Now!" Evy sat straight up in disbelief oogle eyeing the darkness. "Where are you, what do you want?" Her voice raspy at the end of her sentence. Out of the darkness steps a woman, skin glowing. At each step, more of her skin and flowing ghostly nightgown crept from the darkness. Every movement she made was elegent. Her thickly sunset long hair flowing over her pale shoulders. Her head bent, so the crown of her scalp shimmered off of Embala's light. In her cradled arms lay a tame rope, made from black sheets. As the length of them caressed the stone floor

Page 207.

sliding from coiled piles to unraveled hope.

"Get Up Evy, there is much to be done, and not a single moment to spare." In disbelief Evy pulled the covers from her shivering legs. As her leg revealed the golden chain, the substance melted to glitter, then a similar wind that picked up the snakemans ash's returned to swiftly steal the glittered chain away, carrying it through the parted curtains out the huge window.

"Astonishing." Evy's lips creasing upward to shine her most brilliant pearly whites. The young woman holding the sheeted rope tilted her head to show those same demonic black eye's and blazing sharp teath inside of her twisted smile. Jumping up, Evy crossed the room barefoot tiptoeing, each step made her wince due to the floor slowly getting colder as the distance between Lorily and herself crept closer. "It is almost time Evy, go find Aiden's body and family at The Towering Twin's Inn. Talk to Little William Shaw and retrieve Aiden's golden styth medallion." Her head jerked up, neck cracking as if it were broken. "My clothes are gone, I have no way to find the inn, or help when all will be servaying the lands for me, I will once again be an escaped fugitive." "Sh....., All will be well."

Page 208.

Lorily's hands snapped up, dropping the coiled sheets on the floor with a low thump. Both palms on Evy's face, Lorily took her thumbs and brushed them across Evy's eyebrows. Then lorily's fingers burned into Evy's scalp. Before undieing pain shot through her scalp Lorily whispered.

"I had not planned to show you this till after your quest, but the circumstances permit you to gain ever rememberance knowledge of your journey through the past."

Ice slid under Evy's skin, throwing chills up and down her body. Black pain erupted from Evy's thudding brain.

Chapter Sixty One,
Past; Present; No Future?

With The smell of something delicious roaming about the room. The fall sun creeping up Evy's pillows warming her up. A spell of wind blew in through the opique curtains. Evy's head no longer ached, her body felt different, like she was a different version of herself. Evy jumped up, gliding swiftly toward the door, passing a golden mirror. Something made Evy stop and retrace her steps. Evy came back to the mirror in a cautious mood. Looking at herself almost made Evy jump out of her skin. Black engulfed her demonic looking eye's as Evy's lips and face contorted almost disfigured.

"Remember,

Remember!"

The Mirror whispered.

Page 210.

Evy's face soon changed back to hers, except now they have alot of untame freckles and her eye's shone crystal blue with a misty shadow overcast. Chills fled up Evy's spine, reminding her that this was certainly De Ja Vu. Soon after Evy ran out of the room down some dark wood panneled steps toward the dinning room, led by her empty stomach. Evy entered at a sprinters speed, tumbling into a man. They fell to the floor. The weight of her body crushing into his soft muscles, his soft ember eye's gazing passionatly back into her's. Evy couldn't begin to understand why when she rested her eye's upon his, the feeling of butterflyes fluttering to the surface of her skin while making Evy's cheeks blister red. Just then Evy realized that she was in her night shift, white and nearly see through. Now Evy was intensly emberrassed. He hadn't even noticed that about Evy. He lifted his right hand and brushed her hair away from her eye's and tucked them behind her ears.

"Well. Hello there." He whispered up at Evy. As soon as Evy started to smile coyly down at him, The room began to spin. everything shifted to a great blur. When it all stopped, Evy was pleasently seated on a sofa chair, in the study while strange people were talking to her. Evy'd night shift turned into a blue evening gown. her hair pinned up with a patite ribbon of turquoze. Page 211.

"Lorily, Your father Alfred and I have some great news and we wish you to listen and be content. Please understand our grand excitement."

"Nah, Laura. Tis a splendid time to be joyous. Our little Lorily Mcgee has found a willing suiter in Martin O'conner. Whom has asked for your hand in marriage."

Shock fled across Evy's face as she was thrust into her mind and easily played her words over her own conscious tongue. "Pa, Ma. This cannot be. Martin O'conner is the riches and most handsome batchelor in all of Ireland. I have never set my eye's upon his most angelic form. Why should someone of royal stature want to marry a nobody like me?" "Tis a blessing child, One must not question his most holy lord, but understand and be greatful for his loving kindness." "Father, Mother. I have no dowery, we are but a poor family whom tends to our farm." Before Evy was able to add anymore, everything around her spun. Evy was still unsure of what was to come. Evy's heart was pounding so fast as she was trying to not to show her emotions. Lights spun fast then haulted to a pause. candled chandeler's light the ball room and it's eligant guests. fancy dresses glided across the cold floor. A band of musicians played slow romantic melody's.

Page 212.

All this was too much for Evy to understand. Evy headed for the terace and patiently waited under the sillouhette of the stars and clouds that kissed the moon goodnight. her lime gown flowing in the sweet fall wind.

Foot falls crept up behind her, Evy thought about turning and decided to ignore them. A man in a white mask dressed in black stepped onto the terace and stood next to her.

"Nice night, tonight." He started to say. "Tis a fine night." Evy said then presumed to pay close attention to the beauty in the darkness. "Let me tell you a story Miss Lorily McgGee." Evy turned toward him and was now paying attention more attentivly. How did this tall dark and handsome stranger know her name. He continued. "A little while ago, a prince decided to take a strole through the meadows. Upon this most glorious day, he happened to stumble upon a most angelic sight. A beautiful maden working near the moore's near the forest. Collecting wood and fresh fruit for her family. Some way into working, this gracious goddess got exhausted and decided to take a dip in the pond. A grand attempt at solitary peace and a little fun." He stopped for a moment reviling in the story he was telling. Stepping closer to face Evy, continueing more attently.

Page 213

"The spring water carressed the filth from her form. As she stumbled to the shore, Poseiden himself would have marveled at her beauty. So this man followed her as if he were in a trance, when she arrived home, he asked the servents to the poorly farm house about her."

Now his ember eye's shimmered under the light from the sky. he was standing but a foot away. Evy's eye's concentrating on his story and his coy little smile that got larger as he was finishing up his story.

"And since then, Lady Lorily McGee. I have been in Love with you."

Evy's legs almost gave in to swooning as she was mystified by his story. He stepped even closer to her, bending low under the night stars and tried to kiss her. Almost a hairs breathe away from kissing Evy. Something stopped him, it was her hands gently carressing his chest, holding him from consuming all of her."No, I cannot kiss you. Dearest stranger. See I am mystified at your poetics, but I am to be married, and my suitor wouldn't be pleased with how forward you have been toward me."As Evy turned to walk away, he grasps her wrist and yanks Evy back in his arms. Holding tight and kissing her more passionatly then he could have promised."What if I were to tell you, I am your betrothed."

Page 214.

Lips smuldered in heat.

"You promise me heaven and put me through hell."

Everything spun again, glimpses of the night before spun around Evy's cranium, filling it full of wonders about the night they spent before. All night until the fall sun crept over the tree's lighting up the morning sky. Things changed then stopped as Evy was being led up a pathway in a white gown with a lime colored plaid scarf wrapped around her shoulder toward her waist.

Page 215.

on top of the cliff sat a little white marbled church. Leaves flung around the grass and some flew over the cliff's edge, dodging the rocks and being rocked by the oceans untame currents. the sky filled full of angry clouds. and a wind picked up. A few lightning bolts scattered through out the sky. Evy entered the church and a thought crept up to her. If today was supposed to be a blessing from our heavenly lord and his arch angels, then why would it rain. such things were ment to be seen as bad omens. As Evy looked up at the alter, Martin O'conner, stood. Arms open wide and smile gleeming, Nothing to hide. Evy knew from the first time she saw him, that fateful day she ran into him, that Evy would never love anyone else but him. As Evy stepped up to the Alter, she reached her hand toward his gentle fingers and held with much love coming from her heart. The guests settled and the church was filled full of silence. Then the Prior started the ceremony. When Evy's part came and she said her vows, he asked if anyone had any objections. Silence led by A huge electrical volt that crashed down on the church and cut it in half. The floor split, falling open. The front half of the church was in crumbles, the alter pulled from the rest of the cliff. hanging in mid air. nothing but dried roots holding the bottom together. As the ground let loose, Evy began to fall. Martin grasped her hand and tried to pull her up.

But Evy whispered "I love you Martin O'conner". then another bolt startled Martin so bad that he dropped Evy down into the crevice of the cliff. As Evy entered the sliver, a hole emerged and swollowed her whole. Evy woke up in a jungle island. Then all began to blur.

A voice pressed images into her mind, filling Evy's most unanswered questions.

"Evy, Now you must begin your quest."

Chapter Sixty Two;
Bad Name.

Lorily's breath turned to ice as it brought Evy back to reality. No longer did Lorily's fingers hurt Evy's temples. She rubbed her icy hands down Evy's cheeks then bent unhumanly fast letting off alot of unnatural cracking sounds as she picked up the black coiled sheets. Handing them to Evy. She smiled once more and said. "Good luck Evy Trinity Bridgewater." "Thankyou Lorily Mcgee." She thrust them out of the bay window. Then slowly backed away from Evy, into the darkness. Slowly Lorily faded into the peaceful shadows. Then a small cracking sound lifted up and a tiny light shot from the fireplace and headed out the window and headed up to Eldor.

Evy was mystified and full of questions, but brushed them away and continued on with her quest for Ashton.

Page 218.

Evy slid down the sheets toward the unsuspecting servant at the base of the material. Evy knocked her off her feet and into unconsciousness. Not wanting to be recognized Evy borrowed the girls robe and covered her untame curles and then gently moved the girl away from the rope further into the shadows. Evy appologized then went on her way.

Half way to The Towering Twins Inn, Evy ran into a old peddler named Thomas Avery. He was kind enough to share what little food he had with her, and point her in the right direction, Evy thanked him and left in a hurry. Sure that someone was on her trail. It took Evy all day until the following night to find the small town of Shreve Grove. The pathway Evy took split into two seperate paths. One leading to the right headed for a red barn full of calm sleeping animals. The path leading left, crept up to a sign being held up by two lances attatched to a couple of knights. then a small barely lit two story cabin stood sadly behind it. Evy walked up to the door, but was stunned to find it cracked open with small chance of help. Evy turned to leave but was stopped by a meager voice. "Wait miss, can I help you?" Evy turned to see a small toe headed boy, seriously wanting to help anybody in distress. "Is this The Towering Twins Inn?" His eye's lit up. "Yes ma'am, This is. How may I help you?"

Page 219

Evy glanced down bashful.

"I came to mourn, for the loss of General Aiden Mctavish."

The little boy put his finger to his lips and rushed to the cracked door and haulered in.

"Have to go check on the animals, be back in a little while pa."

Then he rushed back to Evy. "My name is Little William Shaw, follow me please, ma'am." Evy shook his hand and told him her name. His eye's lit up as he marveled at who he thought Evy was. After chatting up the journey, he stopped at some old black rust iron creaky gate doors. drenched in untame vines. "Follow the pathway up to the last stone, don't stray from it, or you will be forever lost. He is at the end of the dirt path at the top of the hill." He gave Evy a hug for luck then handed her two lush blood red wild roses and left her at the iron gate in bewilderment. Each mosulim was covered in deep vines and dirty mildew. The higher Up the path Evy went through this laberynth of tombstones and mosulims, fog eloped everything. clouds covered the moon. Evy's legs began to get tired and cold as she reached the top. Covered deeply, Aiden's stone shimmered in what light crept through the wholes in the clouds. "Aiden Mctavish, I am so sorry for everything." Evy fell to her knees and hunched over the now

Page 220.

broken roses. The thornes digging into her skin. Evy fell onto her hands, not caring for the pain. Tears escaped her eye's and drenched from the pedals of the dying roses to the gravel at the base of the stone. The earth started to shake knocking Evy off balance and onto her butt. blue light erupted for a moment at the place where Evy dropped the roses and her tears and blood. The ground shook again. This time Rain poured heavily, and the foggy mist covered up the ground. Out of the ground burst one hand, pulling it to the surface. The other limb was a claw that helped dig it out. Evy almost jumped from her skin. Half rotting corps and half lycan. skin and fur slowly seeping from the bones and falling into disguesting piles of mesh before her eye's. Evy rushed to her feet turning to run. The monster laughed, then pulled at his right eye. Yanking it from it's eye socket and dragging the left eye into it's skull and out of the right socket. As the beast laughed some more, he spun the two eye's in a circle. Flying in mid-air the rope split barbed spikes out and goo ee flesh splattered off of the balls then more spikes popped out from the eye's. Evy was knocked off her feet by a force and pain she couldn't explain. As it hit, Evy fell and rolled down the hill, sliding through mud and weed's knocking into shallow tomb stones until a concrete fence broke her fall and Evy hit her head. Dazed Evy tried to catch her breath.   Page 221.

Rain hit harder and faster. Down the hill crept the half morbid monster man. The smell so intense and nasty that Evy could barely catch her own breath.

"You killed me Evy, How could you be so cruel. I died for your dishonesty and treatchorious motives, You backstabing wentch."

Tears filled Evy's eye's, how could he. What ever he is, speak to me so cruely. The eye's wrapped around Evy's legs, dug into her skin. The smell of blood lingered into the air. His nose twitched as hunger lifted his smile.

"Yum, you smell delicious."

He bent low, then pranced ontop of Evy, ready to dig into her flesh and feed it's despicable monstrious appitite.

Page 222.

Chapter Sixty Three;
Darkest Honesty.

Glancing up past the monster's shoulder, stood a seven foot white marble angelic statue, arms spread wide. The statue's weapon of choice was a spiked metal lance. resting at a tilted angle near it's feet. Thunder hit hard, blinding Evy. The monster was knocked off of her and thwarted back a couple of feet. Another wet animal of beige fur did the damage. As soon as Aiden's zombie carcus rolled a couple of feet away, The attacker ran to the Marble statue that sat pillared over Evy and borrowed it's spiked weapon. Hitting Aiden smack dab in the center of his chest. The weapon went in one side and was escorted out of his rotting back by his black maggot infested Heart. The weapon finally stopped a couple of feet away half burried

Page 223.

in the wet grass, lodged in the dirt. The heart held a great and eerie movement from the vibration of the sudden stop.

The beige beast ran at Aiden's body, jumping high and landing his feet on the monsters shoulders, while ripping the head clean off, covering the beige beasts fur in decaying blood. Then Tossing it carelessly onto the spike where it lodged into the skull, in one eye hole and out the next. Blood dripping down the pike to meet the black heart. Where the rain helped the parts disintagrate down the weapon into the wet grassy mud puddles.

The beige beast shook off his fur and the rain that drenched him. Soon he was Iolis again.

He walked toward Evy, his face serious. Evy could almost imagine what would come from his lips. She was to be scowlded. Then he surprised her. "Why would you risk your life for my folly uneducated decisions?" Iolis bent low and reached for Evy's hand to help her up, but then set her sitting upright on the base of that Angelic statue. He reached down and helped unloosen the painful eye cords and spikes sticking into her flesh. Bent low, he looked up at Evy. "Don't you understand, I love you Evy Trinity Bridgewater."

Gently he pulled a golden medallion out of his pocket.

Page 224.

"I love you soo much, that I would give you what you yearn the most in all of Eldor and Embala combined. Aiden's medallion styth and freedom."

He opened up Evy's hand and placed the golden trinket in her palm, then closed Evy's fingers over it. Tears welled up in her eye's.

Page 225

Chapter Sixty Four;
Exhaustive Seizure.

That night, little William Shaw let them take shelter in his family's barn. The rafters creaked all night long, as if the peices of wood that held up the ceiling were sharing laughs and unconspicuous secrets. Rain continued to pound heavily, The musky scent of wood, and animal feed led in staleness. lightening let little light in from the frowlicking storm about the country side. Evy climbed the ladder up to the second floor of the barn, material wet and uncomfortably sticking to her moist and hot skin. Iolis climbed up before her to find a better place for comfort while they were sheltered and safe to keep warm and get some rest.

As soon as Evy hit the top, her eye's rolled behind

Page 226.

her head and Evy fell into a huge pile of hay. Exhaustion over ran every ounce of her muscles. As Evy lay, everything began to swirl. Evy even believed that her body began to twitch.

Chapter Sixty Five;

Destiny Unraveled.

This time, Hazy smoke, white and fluffy swirled around the area Evy was in and beyond. Blue of all shades filled in the spaces of the cloud swirls. When Evy looked Up and down all was clear and empty. A thick layer of flooring kept her from falling through the clouds to her death. Ahead something crawled out of the misty fluffs. Slowly taking form, It was Lorily. Face still disfigured in a demonic way. Hair blood red with a hint of sunset tint. Wearing a flowing white silky nightgown. Behind her sprouted wings of black and white. every other feather was white or black. The tips curled at the ends, making her look like a half angel

Page 228.

half demon half breed.

She took her hands together and blew some black dust at Evy.

"Evy, Take Iolis with you to find The Cuna Pyramids."

Lorily smiled at her. peices of Lorily started to turn to dust as she slowly disintagrated before Evy's eye's.

"Lorily, What if he doesn't know where to look?"

"Evy, go to Eldor, the island of Nori, find the small inhabitants called Norianna's. Then you will be able to find the passageway to The Cuna Pyramids in the deep jungle of the ancient city of palooma."

Evy waved to Lorily as she left. Evy's eye's went black as reality came flooding back to her.

Chapter Sixty Six,

Eldor.

The first person Evy saw when reality flooded back was Iolis, eye's worried with an uptight look upon his face.

"Evy, are you alright. My love, come back to me please."

"I'm fine Iolis."

He helped Evy sit up and she explained how they needed to travel toward Eldor and the mythical island of Nori. Down below, the barn animals made a pursing noise, which caught her attention. Evy flew down those stairs so fast, Evy barely realized that she could have injured herself. Down below sat a beautiful black stallion that filled her heart with tears for the creatures master. Evy

Page 230.

couldn't help but sniffle and drop a few tears. Iolis flew down the stairs just as fast and understood that Evy was taking a personal moment, trying to mourn in private. He took his fingers and wiped her tears away, then they mounted Ithica. Evy stood by Ithica's rear end and rubbed her palms together, light flickered in sparks. Evy rubbed the light into her sides and Those twenty foot black glimmering wings sprout. Then they were off to Eldor. A couple of hours later they met the shield of water. Entering cautiously Evy followed the same path Luci had taken her to The Elvin Requiem Sanctuary. Evy still felt unsure about bringing Iolis with hwe. Deep inside Evy had to trust her gut feeling on him. Evy forgave him of everything he did. But her uncertainty still kept her alert. This time they moved cautiously through the jungle coral, approached the tree entrance. This place still amazed her. The caral plants moved away from the tree door entrance. The door swung open so fast that Evy jumped back in the saddle, startling Iolis and Ithica. Out popped a little elf child with more wood pilled up to his nose, covering his mouth. His eye's were wide with surprise that Evy was back. He dropped the wood, with a clatter they fell to the gravel. He had a little grey beard. He glanced in shock from Evy to Iolis then high skirted it as far away from them as possible. His beard blowing against him as he left view.

Something seemed wrong. Last time they were friendly. Was it Iolis, maybe it was him they were afraid of. They entered the emense cyllinderic room, Evy's mouth dropped, she was still mystified by the wonderious beauty of it all. The same little elvish man sat staring jubulently at her with his magnificent neon purple eye's. He slowly stopped combing his beard and reading his scrolls to help them.

"Ah, mistress. what have we here?, how may I help you?"

"Well, where to begin?"

He jumped up really fast, his neon purple eye's focusing as if someone had just comanded him to be hospitable and what to say next. With a twinkle in his eye.

"Mistress, no time to waist, we have much to be done here."

Then he talked about The Cuna Pyramids and the norianna's on the island of nori. The ancient pillar civilization of Palooma. Hidden in an ancient hole, revealing a jungle that led to The Cuna Pyramids."

"What do I do with the key's, I'm nervious about everything."

"Tis only natural, Mistress. Reach your hands up to my small fingertips and I shall help you."

Evy reached up to him. Iolis grasped her other hand and Ithica for their suspenseful journey.

Page 232.

Everything swirled, then they were on the white beach, crystal waters, and the waterfall ingulfed in jungle plants.

Page 233.

Chapter Sixty Seven;

Norianna's

The further they went, Evy realized that she was once here before. Up ahead stood a once empty little abandoned village, with food that burned above the fire pits. as they entered through the clearing. something moved fast. small creatures with huge feet that took up their bodies. their eye's were demonic ungulfed in black. and they had huge little white mustaches and abnormal sized noses. they were bald and but a foot wide and high from the ground. they moved fast and were vertually silent. Evy stopped and kneeled low to sit and wait for one to come to her. unsure, if this was what she was supposed to be doing. patience was most certainly a virtue and worth the wait. One hopped from the jungle weeds to rest next to Evy's knee's which she was sitting on. Evy reached her hand out and it hopped onto her open palm like a little bird.

Page 234.

"Are you a Norianna?, where can we find The Cuna Pyramids?"

The creature whispered..."Go to the ancient pillar civilization of Palooma, It's deserted now, but all you have to do is head back to the dead tree and wait for a sign. if you hear a festering creek, then step on that spot and it will lead you to the secret passage. "Evy sat the small Norianna down, thanking him politely. Iolis gave her a sideway's glance of uncertainty. Then they treked up the hill passing the village of the norianna's. The tree was just as lonely as Evy remembered it before. But this time Evy was ready for anything. Iolis walked around the dead tree, branches twisted in agony. Evy stood at the base listening for a festering creek. slowly the sound got larger. Then..."Crack!!"The ground under Evy's feet let loose and down she went. Not before Iolis grasped onto her by wrapping his arms under hers. holding Evy above a hole in the ground. She looked below to see more jungle life and a lava lake wrapping around the island directly below them. Iolis whispered.."Are you ready, close your eye's." He lept upward then they slunk through the hole and landed gently on the surface of the next hidden level of untarnished life below. They settled for a moment, then he let go. Evy turned to see a huge Pyramid towering

Page 235.

above them. Below the surface of the island of Nori, was another world. A lava lake wrapped around the pyramid and jungle life. Iolis wrapped his fingers into her's as they stepped closer to The Cuna Pyramid. Evy pushed the two key peices together and wrapped the stythe under them, tightly securing their hold. In the center of the door sat a place for them. Evy sat them in place then she turned around. Meeting Iolis's lips, crisp and cool against hers. Stepping closer to The Cuna Pyramids, a red scaled dragon circles the outer peremeter of the foundation. While it called for it's mate, the unerving creature's red scales glistened from the lava lake light. The saddle empty, an unusual diversion. Pushing the key peices and the medallion styth further into the wall. With a groaning creek it opens. Air floods in. Inside spirit's and their mates danced, blue ecto plasms attatched like simese twins or ancient difformaties. each dancing in the empty spaces. dozens upon dozens of these floating jubulent creatures swirled neon robyn egg blue, with a hint of ectoplasm white. Evy step in and turn to find Iolis, eye's sad. Evy touched her lips to remember the soft icy kiss they just shared moments before. Evy's eye's swell up with a hint of pain. Evy knew she would never see him or this place again, yet He was apart of her. even if Lorily had to split him in half to give her a fighting chance at happyness. yet it could, would have never been possible.

Page 236.

A shadow creeps behind unsuspecting Iolis, Hiding behind the Kings emense form. The hidden person uses his left hand to grasp onto Iolis's head. Fingers digging into knotts as he yanks even tighter. His right hand lifts a black metalic dagger up to Iolis's neck and slices through his flesh and bone to tear it off into oblivion. He does it so fast that part of the spine is still attatched to the head and they fall and roll through the jungle bush's, down a slope where the lava feasts on his form.

Sire Ahckmelutra leaps over him before he roll's. Leaping for Evy's hand. But only gets dissapointment as a blue glow engulfs her. The last thing Evy remembered is the stone wall closing and everything going white.

Waking up on the old dirt brown sofa in the study.

Page 237.

The Title Of A Crucified Innocence.

Chapter Sixty Eight;
Panic.

Evy wake's up with her heart beating fast, Panic written all over her face. She glances down at the meager book resting in her lap. large black binding overstretched across her wet lap. Inside ancient pictures, she picks it up and turns to the first chapter and finds an illistration of the study. with her seated upon the couch and her brother climbing up on boxes. Every memory flooded back to her. She jumped off the couch and tossed the book across the room to hit the wall and seep down the bricks to the floor under the desk.

A cold sweat dampens her uniform, which consists of a white shirt, her cotton blue sweater, and grey skirt.

Page 238.

worried she jumps up and pulls the burgandy carpet up off the floor to reveal no trap door. She then turns to the desk and search's for the key and flashlights. something crawls up her hand, but this time she is ready and pulls it out and unravels the ribbon. She sticks Alfie back in the drawer. Marveling at the key and how she knew it was there. Quickly she pockets the key and flashlight. She pulls the desk from the wall for another glance at that aweful book. Flashing a light on the cover she soon realizes that it's The Odyssey. Confused, she calls out to Ashton, no response. Evy leaves the room to search for Ashton. Hears him complaining of pain from the fall he took off the boxes stacked up like stairs near the armoir. She finds him in the hallway, sitting on the banister to the grande white stairs. The maid Mrs. Scorcese pats Ashton on the back and sends the siblings on they're way. Evy rush's Ashton and hugs him deeply. "Oh, Ashton. I have missed you so." He pulls back from the embrace face twisting to a comical expression. "Evy, I have only been away from the room for about five minutes. Before that we have been in the study together. Was that book by homer to frightening for your taste. You seemed to fall asleep minutes before my fall. I swear that I thought you were going to wake up and assist me, but I understand

Page 239.

you were embersed in the verses of old text. You were barely snoring. I can say Evy, that when I was looking out the window of the study, I found a perfect way out of this manor. But we must leave while it is still raining and catch the first cargo ship out of London."

"Ashton, could we leave for America, I have always wanted to go there?"

He pulled back in for another reassurring hug, whispering.

"Of course dear sister, I would take you away from your arranged marriage to Sir Henry Lockhart. You should never have to marry without love or of knowledge of who you are marrying."

Evy handed Ashton the key but kept the Lavender ribbon for her hair. Ashton rushed back to the room for Alfie and then met Evy by the backdoor of the manor. They crept from the property headed for The Lattimore Concord Vessel.

Page 240.

Chapter Sixty Nine;
    Starting A New Life.

    The year is 1890 on October the 15th, Ashton and Evy, both 19 years of age. Traveled further west toward the hottest part of the conventional contenent. The sun was up and warm as they passed into an unconspicuious new little town in Utah. Fall leafs fell passionatly from the branches of local tree's in the small town of union town. Barely a strip of old Union town main tied the town together; besides the friendly locals and hardworking miners. Everyone knew everyone. Heat flickered the atmosphere as a damp chilling wind blew through to knock the heat from the blazing sun off course to give the slaving community a breather. Evy applied for the postal service of incoming and outgoing postal.

Page 241.

She was hired from her friendly smile and jubulent demeaner. Ashton aquired a job at the local union town copper mine near the union town mountain bend. Both worked steady jobs and saved up for a little piece of property near town. A two level house with two bedrooms a walk in closet and a basement for carnal storage space. The house had green siding and a metal fence that stretched around the property and the three storage sheds. She loved the house for the three tree's that grew from nothing. Two little apple tree's in back and a huge jungle tree that kept the house cool during summer. Attatched to the back door, sat a little brown porch. The porch up front held two colums of white attatched to an open half wall for privacy. The pathway was dingy from careless owners before. An old dirt path led out the gate to the right up toward old magna main. Tree's overlapped the few houses on the block. above few clouds lingered in fall slumber. One september day a cowboy brings her a letter. His skin ruggid, his hair wild and untame in different shades of beige and dark brown. With eye's of emerald with blue shooting from the centers of his corneas. Fireworks. He hands her the letter, she notices the gentle graze of stubble from his jaw line and can't help but be mesmerized. Something about him makes her feel light headed.

She open's it and reads..

Page 242.

"Dearest Lady Evy Trinity Bridgewater,
I have traveled across ocean's
and deep deserted landscapes for
your hand in marriage.
Please do me the
honor of marrying me.
Sir Henry Lockhart." Evy glances up from the letter,
noticing that he was suddenly gone. confussed she puts the letter down and
finds the gentleman on the wood porch of the postal block on union town main.
Knealing, in his right hand he holds up a small exquisite sterling silver ring
with diamonds incrusted in the silver. His left hand he held his hat to his
chest. The look in his eye's begged for her to answer his question. She hardly
knew him, yet everything about him felt familiar. She was ready to settle
down, and start a life with this man of mystery. they have a lifetime for
experiencing eachother and growing together. She said yes. The postal shop
closed at 7pm sharp. Henry politely walks Evy to the house, she shares with
Ashton, ready to say good evening. The sky black, grey, silver red and white.
Above an opening of tree's sit's Sire Ahckmelutra's face surrounded by
clouds. "You can never escape me Evy, You are rightfully mine!" Evy holds
tight to the white metal bannister on

Page 245.

the porch, her legs being pulled up into the storm. Evy's fingers turning white. Then she lets go, but Henry grasps onto her arms holding her for a split second, his eyes full of confussion and shock as he can clearly see that the sky has a man talking in plain view. Henry's arms give and Evy slips out and is sucked into the face of the storm.

Page 244

Chapter Seventy;
        Heavenless Peace.

        Evy woke up in the fetal position on a stone cold floor, her hair was wet from the storm, her navy blue gown was moist. Evy was absolutly chilled to the bone. Dizzyness crept into her conscious. Evy was unsure of this new place she was in. How was this all real, Evy checked the maroon carpet in the study and the trap door was gone. How was this even possible from the begginning. Evy was a pawn in this chess game from hell. Was this her punishment for some undescribable crime she commited in a past life. Light danced in flickered jubulence about the room from dozens upon dozens of candles. Every surface held

                        Page 245.

a little wax instrument of light. A huge meca of candles rested on the mantle above the blazing warm fireplace.

Evy sat up and tried to reach for the pedestal in order to raise herself to her feet. Evy grabbed it for balance. Sire Ahckmelutra jumps from behind the pedistal, startling her. He grasps onto Evy, they begin to wrestle, but the water on her skin from the storm makes her slippery.

Ahckmelutra lept one final time to grab Evy, she jumped back to avoid his vile fingers, only to tumbled out the window of the tower. Falling down onto rough cliff rocks that crack bones in her neck, paralizing her suddenly. Down below the rushing ocean spurts wash Evy's body into the water where she may now lay in peace.

Away from the sorrow.

Or So She Thought.

Fin.

Page 246.

246

Hello, my name is Sherianne Duffy, i was born on october 15th in slc, utah. happily married to the love of my life Mr. king, on october 31st 2012, have a beautiful little boy named dean, a wonderful 18year old pitbull chow named angel mama's. my inspiration is from my grandmother, who worked 2 jobs and other sides chores be it illegal, that kept us off the streets when the state took us and she was rewarded us. i am greatful for her and my uncle jesse who took me and my brother in and raised us in a poor home for 20 years. she is my hero. my mother helped shape my imagination by telling stories and taking me on night walks. which i continue through to today. the illistration of the couple holding eachother is something i found on myspace years ago and i give credit to the talented person i will never know who drew it. aiden was created for ian somerholder, from vampire diaries, and iolis was created for jensen ackles from supernatural. i hope one day that peter jackson and tim burton come together to create some movies from my twisted imagination. they would only understand my dark creatures. and most of all thankyou all for being patient and reading my at first boring story. but the novels pick up i promise. join me in my other books. this is only the beginning.:)
sincerly, S.A.D. (c)

Book 1- The Title Of A Crucified Innocence

Book 2- Prince In The Mirror

Book 3- Wylers Waterdweller Secrets

Lightning Source UK Ltd.
Milton Keynes UK
UKHW050716050521
383113UK00002B/180